I0699651

BOBBY

LORD OF ACTON WATERS

William Smock

ATOPON BOOKS

Atopon Books
907 15th Street
Santa Monica, California 90403
United States

Publisher's Cataloging-in-Publication data

Name: Smock, William, author.
Title: Bobby, Lord of Acton Waters / William Smock.
Description: Santa Monica, CA: Atopon Books, 2024.
Identifiers: LCCN: 2024931470 | ISBN: 979-8-9866109-1-7 (paperback) /
979-8-9866109-2-4 (hardcover) / 979-8-9866109-8-6 (ebook)
Subjects: LCSH Coming of age--Juvenile fiction. | Middle ages--Juvenile
fiction. | Great Britain--History--Juvenile fiction. | Historical fiction.
| BISAC JUVENILE FICTION / Historical / Medieval | JUVENILE
FICTION / Boys & Men | JUVENILE FICTION / Humorous Stories |
JUVENILE FICTION / Social Themes / Adolescence & Coming of Age
Classification: LCC PZ7.1.S66 Bo 2024 | DDC [Fic]--dc23

Cover illlustration by the author.

Printed in the United States of America.

Table of Contents

This is a story about the naughtiest boy in the world. What makes him so rude, so mean and unbearable? At the age of 11 he is the ruler of a tiny realm. He can do whatever he pleases.

Can anything or anyone turn Bobby into a decent human being? Could he ever become the hero of this tale? Read on. The year is 1147. Bobby is an earl. He has a castle, a village and the countryside round about. All the land in England belongs to a few hundred nobles like Bobby. And all the farmers belong to the landowners. They work for the lord, handing over half of what they grow. They are also the soldiers in the lord's army.

Most lords cared about their subjects and tried to keep them happy. Not Bobby.

Chapter I. The Young Earl

The sun rose. A stained glass window splashed brilliant colors across Bobby's room. Feeling the sun on his face, he woke up. Yawning, he pulled on his velvet robe, his crown and his fur slippers.

"Breakfast!" he shouted. A servant crouching outside the door rushed down to tell the kitchen that Bobby was up.

Bobby slept in a tower high above his castle. He threw open the window and surveyed his domain. He could see beyond the castle grounds to his village, his fields and pastures, his forests and the blue hills beyond. It was summer. There was a soft buzz of insects. Morning sunlight caught them flittering in the air.

The door flew open. Servants rushed in with trays of food and drink. "What would your Lordship . . . ?" asked one.

"Raspberries, hot cross buns with lots of butter, and a songbird grilled on a stick."

"Right away, my Lord," said the servant. "In the meantime, please have some soft-boiled quail eggs, waffles, sausages and honey." Bobby tucked a big white napkin under his chin. The servant flew back down the stairs.

Bobby never took a bath. He never even washed his hands unless they were sticky. If anyone even hinted there was dried oatmeal on his chin, he threw a tantrum. He was a nice-looking boy, with brown hair and brown eyes. But his brow was usually twisted in exasperation, his chin was usually lifted in disdain, and his voice had a whiny edge.

Bobby's huge wolfhounds, Alf and Bagger, woke up and stretched. They romped up the stairs, scattering the servants. The servants were used to it. Bobby gave each dog a waffle. The servants, who had never tasted a waffle, shook their heads in disbelief.

After breakfast Bobby went down to the Great Hall. There he found his parents, his sister, his teacher, his Jester, his Master of the Horse, his Master of the Hounds and several other Masters.

"Bobby, will you go to school today?" asked Lady Nelda, his mother.

"What for?"

"You should learn to read and write. You're eleven years old," she replied.

"Can *you* read and write?"

"Yes," said his mother. "Reading is my hobby."

"Good!" said Bobby. "Read to me." They had this conversation every day.

"How come *I* have to go to school?" groaned Bobby's sister Alison. She was 13. She was straight and slender, with blonde hair falling to her shoulders. She had a pinched, severe look. Her dress was a washed-out blue, her hair dull and uneven.

"Because we make you," explained Lady Nelda. "We can't make Bobby. He's the earl."

Bobby had inherited the title from his uncle. He outranked his own father. He was top dog in Acton Waters.

"Make me, then," said Alison. Lady Nelda drew in her breath.

"Cut off her pigtails," suggested Bobby in a bored tone of voice.

The Jester tried to lighten the mood. "When is a dog the ruler?" he asked.

"When he's a little bored," answered Bobby. He already knew the joke.

"Bobby!" said his father boldly, "You *must* go to school!"

"Dad, *you* must go horseback riding till suppertime," said Bobby. And that's what his father did. He took along the Jester, who was good company.

Now the Masters stepped forward.

"Wanna go riding, Milord?" asked the Master of the Horse.

"Wanna shoot bow and arrows?" asked the Master of the Hounds.

"Wanna kick around an inflated pig's bladder?" asked the Sports Master.

"Wanna learn to play the hunting horn?" asked the Bandmaster.

"Wanna play with girls?" asked the Dancing Master.

"Wanna play with boys?" asked the Taskmaster.

"I guess I'll ride my pony. Then I'll play with my toy soldiers. Then I will hunt squirrels."

Bobby went to the stables. The Master of the Horse brought out Bobby's spirited gray pony. The two riders set off across the countryside, the Master staying well behind.

The morning was warming up. Bobby rode through a pasture where cows and their calves were nibbling grass. He rode into a wood where leafy branches swayed in the wind. He came to a pond where mother ducks were schooling their ducklings.

He rode to the top of a little hill. He could see his castle in the distance. He could see women doing laundry in the stream. He could see men weeding rows of grapevines, digging beets and planting carrots.

"Like a bite to eat?" asked the Master of the Horse from a polite distance.

"I do feel like an apple," admitted Bobby. So he had one.

Bobby rode under a rugged cliff, through a deep valley, around a marsh with otters in it, back to the castle. The castle was not fortified; England's civil wars never threatened it.

The village and its surrounding farms were just big enough to support an earl and his family. No one else wanted it.

Bobby's castle was a big stone house with a turret at one corner. It had twenty rooms or so, most of them empty. The biggest room, where the family spent most of its time, was as big as a small church. Ivy grew up the outside; it turned a beautiful shade of red in fall. A rolling lawn surrounded the house, dotted with oak trees. A flock of sheep kept it trimmed. A stream wandered through the grounds. It provided splashing opportunities to children and fishing holes for grownups.

In Bobby's huge sandbox the Taskmaster had arranged 700 toy soldiers. There were toy castles, bridges, villages, lakes and streams. Toy trees, cows and horses, boats and wagons. Bobby divided his men into two armies and started a war. He made crashing noises with his voice, pretending the men were killing each other. By the end he was sweeping his hands across the rows of soldiers, mowing down dozens at a time. He left several hundred fallen soldiers for the Taskmaster to put away.

Then he went to the armory to find the Master of the Hounds. He shot arrows at squirrels in the big oak trees on his grounds. He missed. The Master of the Hounds killed two or three and Bobby took them to the Cook.

It was soon supper time, so he sat down to a dinner of barbecued chicken, roast beef, meat loaf, fried squirrel, mashed turnips and salad, followed by cakes and puddings. An orchestra played some of his favorite tunes and his sister sang a song or two. She didn't mind missing dinner. She was a vegetarian. She gave most of her food to the badgers in the woods.

After dinner the Cook came out. "Everything okay?"

"Meat loaf is just garbage, in my opinion," said Bobby. Alison smiled in secret agreement. The cook bowed and backed out.

Bobby had a few friends. Boys from the village – Piers, Kenward and Emonds – were paid to play with him. They weren't allowed to win. When they wrestled, Bobby ended up on top. When they raced Bobby came in first. In return for losing, the boys got hearty meals in the kitchen – roasts, casseroles and desserts far better than anything they got at home. In winter they were given fur vests so they could play in the snow with Bobby.

Bobby ordered people to do what he wanted. But some things he couldn't control. One was the weather. He had a fit whenever it rained.

From time to time there were visitors who were nobler than he was. They wouldn't take orders. This made Bobby so mad that he would run outside and stomp the flowers his gardeners had just planted.

He couldn't control his health, either. In those days doctors weren't much good, so Bobby got measles, mumps, diphtheria, chicken pox, and whooping cough. A sore throat made Bobby so mad that he swore, using curses he had overheard farmers using on balky oxen. This shocked his mother, flustered his father, and irritated his sister. She was not allowed to swear.

Bobby was in love with a village girl named Bronwen. She was blonde, tall and 19. Though he ordered her to love, honor and obey him, she wouldn't. When he asked her to play she just laughed and shook her head. When he chased her she stopped, turned around and threw him roughly to the ground. When he said he would have his soldiers beat her up she said saucily, "That would probably make me love you a lot, Bobby." Bobby got so mad he would spit on any dog or cat he saw.

Chapter II. The Tunisian Beggarman

Bobby first heard about the beggarman from a villager. "We're having a dance on the green, My Lord, after work on Saturday," the man reported.

"I'll send my orchestra," offered Bobby.

"No need," said the man. "There's a Tunisian beggarman in town. Brown as a nut. He's unbelievable on the guitar."

"You're kidding, right?" asked Bobby, wondering how a beggarman could be better than his own professional musicians. He decided not to go. Bronwen would be sure to dance every dance with Pete, her boyfriend.

When he got the mumps a week or so later he heard about the beggarman again. Bobby's doctor said mournfully, "I've done everything I can, my Lord. I pressed your forehead with nettle roots. I made you a bitter drink of dried berries. Now we have to wait."

"Bah!" said Bobby. "You worthless fart!"

"Shall I bring the Tunisian beggarman?" asked the doctor. "He's done marvelous things down in the village. He cured Dame Edith's stomach ache. He stopped Deacon Elmslie's bad dreams and most of Little Buddy's bed wetting."

"All right," said Bobby. "Get the beggarman." But the beggarman didn't come.

The next time he heard about the beggarman was at dinner one night, when his sister blushed and said, "I have dreams about the Tunisian beggarman. He is tall and handsome. He has gleaming white teeth. He sings like a nightingale and he is a gifted doctor. Although he is probably older than me, I doubt he is over 18."

Bobby replied, "The Tunisian beggarman is about as interesting as my left sock." He was getting jealous. He didn't have much of a singing voice. He couldn't read, he couldn't fence, he couldn't draw. Nobody smiled when he walked into a room. True, he was only 11. He wished he were 18, gifted and fascinating like the beggarman.

The next morning Bobby went down to the village, pretending to look for an arrow he'd lost in the bushes.

Someone tapped him on the shoulder. "Can I help you?" It was a handsome, pale brown man with coal black hair and flashing eyes. There was a guitar slung over his shoulder. He gave Bobby a nice, easy smile.

"No," said Bobby.

"My name is Fahd," said the man, extending his hand. "What's yours?"

Bobby glared up at the man. "I'm the Earl of Acton Waters, buddy, and I don't shake hands with people like you."

"Ah," said Fahd.

"Are you the beggarman?" asked Bobby, even though he already knew the answer.

"Yes I am," said Fahd. "If you need music, doctoring, or fortunetelling, I can help you out. My charges are very reasonable. Even peasants can afford me."

Bobby debated what to answer. "I doubt you're worth a stomped acorn," he finally said.

Fahd laughed in the same carefree way Bronwen did.

"I'll bet you sing like a crying baby," sneered Bobby. The man laughed again.

"I'll bet you couldn't cure a sniffle," said Bobby. The man just smiled.

"I'll bet your fortunetelling is just made up," said Bobby.

The man gave him a sharp look. "You're right about that part," he said.

"I'll bet you have fleas." said Bobby. "I'll bet you don't know your own middle name. I'll bet you can't turn a somersault." Bobby was red with rage.

"How much do you bet?" asked the man.

Bobby, who couldn't even remember what they were betting on, said, "An ounce of gold."

"That's not enough."

"My crown!" said Bobby. "My horse! Everything!"

"All right," said the beggarman.

"What do *you* bet?" asked Bobby.

"My guitar. It's all I've got."

"That's rich," said Bobby. "A guitar for my whole realm . . . people in my earldom will chuckle about this for years to come."

"Who will pick the winner? That is, judge my singing, check for fleas and so on?" asked the beggarman.

"I will," said Bobby. "I call the shots around here."

"That's not fair," said the man. "How about the priest?"

"No!" said Bobby.

"Then the deal is off." The man smiled at Bobby and turned to go.

Bobby got so mad he kicked a dog who was napping in the sun. "Get the priest then, you wriggling mealworm!"

The man leaned into a window and spoke to someone. A little boy ran to get Father Anselm. Onlookers started to gather. Bobby just glowered.

When Father Anselm came, the beggarman explained the bet. The priest looked sadly at Bobby. He knew that sensible advice would not get through.

The beggarman turned a somersault. He went behind a bush, took off his clothes and asked Father Anselm look for fleas. "Clean," said the priest. Father Anselm wasn't afraid to tell the truth, even though Bobby rarely listened to him.

"My middle name is Gamal," said the beggarman. He turned to face the villagers. "Is anybody sick?"

An old woman held up her hand. "I have a bad back," she said. He gave her a vigorous back rub. Then he murmured a few words in an unknown language.

"How long is this going to take?" asked Bobby.

"That was it," said the beggarman. Smiling at the woman, he asked, "How do you feel?"

"I haven't felt this good in 20 years!" She leaped into the air and kicked her heels together. The crowd broke into applause.

The man began to sing. He sang a slow, sad song in his own language. The crowd paid rapt attention. At the end they applauded again.

The beggarman turned to the priest. "Do I yowl like a baby?" Father Anselm shook his head. "Could I cure a case of sniffles?" The priest nodded. The man turned to Bobby. "Well?" he said.

Bobby took off his crown and threw it in the dirt. "You're the earl and I'm a homeless stranger. But I don't care, so I won anyway!" And he strode off toward the forest. The people watched in amazement. The only sound was the rustling of leaves in the treetops and a distant crow, cawing.

"Wait!" called Fahd, running after Bobby. "What does an earl do? Can he wander the world, sing and help people?"

"Of course not," said Bobby. "He has to stay here and run things."

"Can he seek out the girl of his dreams?"

"Of course not," said Bobby. "He has to marry a woman of high rank, chosen by his family."

"What's your family like?"

"Stupid," said Bobby.

Fahd tried to picture them. "Well," he said dubiously, "let's go and meet them."

"Go see for yourself," said Bobby. "I'm a beggarman. You're the earl." And he headed out of town with a grim, determined look on his face.

Fahd put on the crown and walked toward the castle. Alison was in the Great Hall, daydreaming. Seeing the crown on Fahd's head, she threw her arms around his waist. "Oh, are you noble? Will you marry me? Oh, I'm so happy! Thank you so much!"

"I'm sorry," said Fahd. "I'm too old. I think I'm your brother now anyway." Alison gasped and ran to her room.

Hearing the commotion, Lady Nelda came out of her sewing room. "Yes?" she said.

"I'm Fahd, the new earl. I won the crown from Bobby in a bet."

"You did?" A gleam came into Lady Nelda's eye. "Will you be generous to your subjects and retainers?"

"Yes," said Fahd.

"Will you be worthy of the name Acton Waters?"

"I hope so," said Fahd.

"Will you go to school?"

"I'm afraid not." said Fahd. "I'm 25."

Lady Nelda had run out of questions. Just then Bobby's father got back from his day of fishing. She took him aside and whispered, "This man is the new earl. He won the earldom in a bet. His name is Flawed."

Bobby's father's seized Fahd's hands. "Marvelous! You look like a decent chap! Brown as a shoe!" He strode to the window and threw open the curtains. In sunlight the rugs and furniture looked worn and faded. Even the dogs were going orange around the roots of their hair.

"That's better," said Bobby's father. "What game shall we play? Old Maid? Hare and Hounds?"

"I play music," said Fahd.

"Music," replied the father guardedly. "We have an orchestra for that."

There was a long silence. The Jester spoke up. "Why do pigeons coo?"

Silence.

"Because they don't know how to cluck," answered the Jester, waiting for some sign of appreciation.

Bobby's mother winced. Bobby's father squinted into the middle distance. In her room, Alison dreamed sad dreams of loss.

"Do you need any doctoring, fortunetelling, or personal advice?" asked Fahd.

They avoided his eyes.

Fahd took off his crown and handed it to Lady Nelda. "I'll be going, then."

"I'm not sure you understand," said Lady Nelda.

"Why does everyone hate me?" moaned Alison into her pillow.

"Let's start over," said Bobby's father.

But Fahd was gone.

Chapter III. The Road

Fahd went loping down the road after Bobby. Before long he spotted him picking wild blackberries. Bobby looked up warily. "What do *you* want?"

"You can have the crown. I prefer begging."

Bobby should have felt relieved. But for some reason he didn't. Fahd was such a cheerful, unselfish person. Bobby felt an unfamiliar urge to make a good impression. "What are *you* going to do?"

Fahd tasted a few berries. "I don't know. Guess I'll hit the road. Find out what's on the other side of the hill. That's what I do."

Bobby studied the clouds. He had never had a plan before. He didn't have one now. "That's what I was thinking, too," he said. Without further discussion the two of them set off, side by side.

The first person they met was a blind old woman, guided by a little girl.

"Good evening, Mother," said the Tunisian beggarman.

"Good evening, Sir. How far to Acton Waters?"

"Not more than an hour. Are you going home?"

"God forbid," said the blind woman. "The lord there is a mean little kid."

"Is he?" said Fahd with a grin. Bobby clenched his fists.

"He treats his dogs better than his servants. And according to my daughter, he smells like a pair of athletic socks."

Bobby addressed her in a choked voice. "Isn't there *something* good about him? I've heard he's bright for his age."

"Well," said the woman reflectively. "He does pay some of the village boys to let him win at games. He's as helpless as a baby."

"Fare thee well, Mother," said Fahd and turned to go. A curse formed on Bobby's lips, but he held his tongue.

They walked and walked through meadows and over streams till they came to a tidy little town called Brown's Landing. Night was approaching. They were hungry and needed a place to sleep. Stopping at a busy corner, the beggarman tuned his guitar. He asked Bobby to pass the hat.

"Me, beg?" asked Bobby in disbelief.

"That's what I do," answered Fahd. "If you won't help, then go ahead without me." He smiled. "But which is worse, asking for money, or squeezing the peasants dry?"

"I own my peasants," said Bobby. "Everything they have is already mine."

"Have it your way." Fahd laid his cap on the ground and struck up a tune. He had a beautiful voice. A circle of listeners formed, and his cap soon filled with coins. Bobby merely watched. Fahd eventually picked up the money, nodded pleasantly to Bobby and went off to find an inn.

The streets were emptying. Bobby didn't know where to go. Just then a man in a fur robe trotted past on a warhorse. It was the earl of the town, Lord Brown. Bobby knew him. "Sandy!" he shouted.

The man looked back but did not stop. "Who are you?"

"Bobby! Earl of Acton Waters!"

"Then I'm a frog's nose," laughed the man, riding off. "Bobby never travels without a squad of archers, a man with a bag of muffins and a girl with a fan!" The man's scornful laugh was still echoing around the square when he disappeared in the distance.

It was getting dark and cold. The townspeople were eating supper. Their windows glowed yellow. Bobby had not brought any warm clothing. He took a deep breath, squared his shoulders, walked up to a door and knocked. A friendly-looking man appeared. Bobby said stiffly, "I am a stranger in this town. I have a lot of money but I forgot to bring it with me. If you feed and shelter me I'll send my servants to pay you in a couple of days."

The man smiled. "This is not an inn. Come join us for dinner. You can sleep with my boys. What's a young lad like you doing out on the road by himself?"

Bobby said he had climbed the hill to see what was on the other side. He was soon by the fire, happily gnawing a roast chicken neck. That night he slept on a hard, narrow bed with two little boys – Pip and Prothero. They wanted to wrestle. Although he was bigger, Bobby let them win. They wanted a story. Bobby had learned plenty of stories from the Jester, but this time he made up one of his own.

"Once there was a boy with everything you could ever want: roast beef with gravy, jewels, servants, dogs, horses, soft feather beds. But the boy wasn't happy. Something was missing."

"Toys?" asked little Pip.

"Cake?" asked Prothero.

"No," said Bobby. "He had those. It was something else."

"Well, what else did he need?" asked the boys.

"I don't know," said Bobby. While he puzzled over this the boys dozed off.

The next day dawned cool and clear. Bobby stepped out onto the High Road, looked both ways and headed north, away from home. Dew was hanging on the grass, catching the sun like diamonds. Birds trilled from the hedgerows. Lambs could be heard bleating to their mothers. After a mile or two Bobby heard a whistle. The Tunisian beggarman was catching up with him. "Find a place to stay? Something to eat?" Bobby nodded. "Without begging?"

"A family took me in. I offered to come back and pay, but they said no."

"Hmmm," said Fahd. "Sounds like begging."

"Maybe it was," conceded Bobby. They walked for a mile or two in silence.

"Know any good stories?" Fahd asked.

"The Little Round Bun."

"I've heard it. Have you heard Chicken Little?"

"About a million times." The day was heating up. Tramping along the road had coated them with dust. A pair of pesky flies buzzed around Bobby's head.

There was a lone traveler on the road ahead. They soon caught up with him, because he had a funny habit of straying into the bushes beside the road, shaking himself, returning to the road and veering off again.

"Good day, Sir," said Fahd, tipping his cap. "A beautiful day for walking."

"Not for me," said the man. "I keep going off to the left."

"Would it help if I took your my arm?"

"No," said the man sadly. "I will just keep aiming to the left anyway. There's a reason for it. Care to hear it?"

"Sure," said Fahd. "We need a good story."

"It's quite a long one," said the man.

"So much the better," said Fahd, and prepared to listen.

Chapter IV. The Man Who Turned Left

"My name is Eldritch," said the man. "I used to be quite an important person, a master magician. I could pull a live rabbit out of a hat. I could find a coin in your ear. It's all fake, of course. There is no real magic and I hope you never thought there was."

Fahd and Bobby shook their heads solemnly, though they both believed in magic.

"Magic is quite an expensive line of work. It calls for a lot of equipment – special playing cards, top hats, mirrors and chests. To buy these things I borrowed money from my dad. He is a blacksmith. I promised to repay him as soon as my magic business took off. Luckily I'm a good magician. I became popular at markets and fairs. I hired assistants – a lovely young brother and sister. I bought a cart and horse. All the money I earned went into the show.

"After a year or so my father needed his money back. 'You are well-known now,' my Dad said. 'At every show you collect more money than I lent you in the first place. I've had a bad year. If I can't find some money I'll have to go out of business.'

"I told him to wait a little longer. I only needed two more things – the special box used to make it look like you're sawing a woman in half, and the basket and swords used in the 'boy in the basket' trick. So I did get the equipment. But then I realized these were old, worn-out tricks. I needed new tricks, never seen before. That costs money – everything I was able to earn.

"I didn't think about my father again until somebody told me he'd sold his blacksmith shop. He was picking fruit and my mother was taking in sewing. I felt so ashamed that I didn't dare go home. I just tried to forget them.

"One day they showed up in a market. I didn't spot them until after the show. They had been standing in the back of the crowd. After everyone else left they were still there, arms folded. I went over to them – 'Mom! Dad!' I pretended I hadn't heard that they lost everything.

"They didn't say anything. My mother began to cry. My father just glared at me. Then he raised his fist and punched me. Blacksmiths are very strong. I turned my head to dodge his blow and his fist landed on my left ear. I fell down, stunned. My parents walked slowly away without saying a word. When I finally got up, I started turning left. And I have been turning left ever since."

Bobby, Fahd, and the man walked along in silence. They went slowly because of the man's steering problem.

It was Fahd who spoke first. "Then what happened?"

"I lost interest in magic. I sold off my cart and equipment for a lot of money. Now I am traveling all over England, looking for my parents."

"What will you do when you find them?"

"I'll give them the money. And I'll ask them to forgive me."

"What if we punched your right ear? Would that straighten you out?" asked Bobby. Fahd gave him a shocked look.

"I hadn't thought of it," said the man.

They reached Beckham, the next town, after many side trips into the bushes. Then the man went to the marketplace to ask after his parents. Fahd got ready to sing.

This time Bobby helped him. At first he was no good at collecting money. When people walked past without contributing, he would glare at them and curse. If they did contribute, he wouldn't thank them. Fahd was too busy to notice.

Gradually Bobby began to see that politeness attracted donations. He began to understand why people are polite. With the money he collected he and Fahd ate and slept comfortably that night.

As he lay on their bed of fresh hay Bobby's mind went back to the magician. His own parents were surely worrying about him. He had just disappeared. He didn't want them coming after him, so he decided to get in touch. He wondered who was running Acton Waters in his absence.

Chapter V. Alison, Countess of Acton Waters

The first night after Bobby's disappearance nobody worried. They thought he was just being naughty – hiding in the stables, spying on Bronwen or trying to stay up all night. The next night, when he still hadn't returned, they started to worry. Even though he was a bad boy, his parents loved Bobby. They blamed themselves, as parents do, for his faults.

"If only we'd been firmer," said Bobby's mother.

"If only he had looked up to his Dad the way other boys do," added his father.

They searched everywhere. Someone thought he'd seen Bobby heading up the High Road. Travelers were questioned, but no one had seen a haughty young earl. Just the usual assortment of merchants, pilgrims, gypsies, beggars and dancing bears.

They looked in the ponds and under the cliffs. They hunted around for kidnappers. But there was no sign of Bobby. People were aware that the Tunisian beggarman had gone off the same day. But everyone knew they were enemies, so it had to be a coincidence.

Acton Waters needed an earl, someone who could give orders and dispense money. Bobby's parents couldn't do it. The previous Earl had ruled them out. Who could it be?

The family finally chose Alison. This choice made sense to people. And the former Earl who picked Bobby would probably have approved.

Her parents worried that Alison was too shy and nervous for the job. But when they told her she had been picked she gave them a jubilant look. The next morning she ordered her parents to go to school. Then she jumped on her horse and rode off across the fields, trampling the farmers' freshly-planted crops.

"I will never bathe or brush my teeth again," she vowed at dinner. "And never again will meat be served." She put her parents to bed right after dinner and stayed up till two. She stopped washing.

Alison outlawed hunting and fishing. Her subjects paid no attention. But at the palace nothing was served but parsnips and Brussels sprouts, weed stew and buckwheat porridge. Alison's parents began looking greedily at mice brought in by the cat. Alf and Bagger, Bobby's dogs, barely touched their bowls of carrot peels. They got thinner and thinner until the Master of the Hunt mercifully gave them away to a passing knight.

Alison began to wear high heels and makeup. She moved into Bobby's turret room. Although she was really too old for dolls, she ordered three big dolls with blond wigs and silk outfits.

Alison thought boys were too rough. She ordered the boys of Acton Waters not to fight or play rough games, to keep their hair combed and throw away their jackknives. The punishment for breaking these rules was a day of silent prayer.

Alison ordered people to bow when she passed. If they didn't, she screeched at her soldiers to beat them up. The soldiers, who lived in the village, promised they would but never did.

Chapter VI. The Vicar of Beckham

Meanwhile, at their latest stop, Fahd and Bobby got up, splashed their faces at the well and ate a hearty breakfast – bacon, eggs, applesauce and crumpets.

Bobby told Fahd he wanted to reassure his parents. "The problem is, I can't let them find out where I am. If I do, they'll come for me."

"Don't tell them. And don't tell anyone here who you are. Give a note to the coachman, and tell him you found it in the road."

"Hmm," said Bobby. "What should I say in the note?"

"You could say, 'Don't worry about me. I'm having some adventures. I'll be back in a couple of years.' Then you could add that you love them."

Bobby squinted. Did love he them? He'd never thought about it. Maybe he did.

Fahd went and found a piece of paper. He borrowed a quill and some ink from the innkeeper and laid it all out for Bobby.

"But I don't know how to write," said Bobby. "I hate school."

"We'll have to hire someone," said Fahd, who was also illiterate. For a halfpenny the innkeeper agreed to do the writing. Here is his note to Bobby's parents:

"Doont orry bot mi. I em torbelen for awle. I ell bee bak en uh cobl eers. I luf eu. I ems eu. Bobe"

The innkeeper read it back to Bobby. It sounded fine. The innkeeper folded it over and addressed it:

"Tu erls partens, Actin Oaters." He read this with Bobby and it sounded perfect. So Fahd gave it, with a penny, to a coachman traveling south. The coachman couldn't read either. He hoped one of his passengers could.

With the happy feeling that he'd done his duty, a feeling he had never had before, Bobby hit the road again. For the first few miles he practiced singing harmony with Fahd. Fahd was teaching him a beautiful song in his language, Arabic.

"It means, 'Wind in the trees, moon in the sky, where is my beloved? The wind leaves no mark on the water, the moon leaves only moving shadows. Is love, too, a mere illusion?'" Fahd took the song pretty seriously, and was angry when Bobby sang the Arabic word for "moon" so it sounded like the Arabic word that means "odor."

After awhile the two caught up with a roly poly man dressed in black. He had a round, smiling face and pink cheeks. They introduced themselves all around.

"I'm from Beckham, the town you just passed. I'm on my way to Effling's Farm to visit an old lady who's sick in bed."

"Are you a doctor?" asked Bobby.

"I'm a vicar," he said. "She'll want me to murmur some prayers. Where are you going?"

"Anywhere and nowhere," said Fahd. "Just traveling."

"I suppose you'll end up in the wars," said the Vicar. "The King is badly short of soldiers. If you make the mistake of walking past the Sheriff of Beckham, you'll probably never see your Mum again."

"How long do you have to stay in the army?" asked Bobby.

"Forever. Until you're killed or crippled. How old are you?"

"Sixteen," said Bobby, lying as he often did. "Do you get to kill people?"

"Oh yes. And they get to kill you," said the Vicar, looking him up and down. "You look about eleven."

"And you look like a painted pig," rejoined Bobby with a smirk.

"I hope you don't say anything like that to the Sheriff," said the Vicar sadly. He picked Bobby up and threw him over one shoulder. Bobby kicked. With one of his giant hands the Vicar squeezed Bobby's ankles together. Bobby sucked in his breath. "Will you take it back?" asked the Vicar calmly.

"No!" gasped Bobby. The Vicar laughed and put him down. Bobby made a mental note that fat people can be very strong.

"I once knew another angry boy," said the Vicar with a smile. "He learned to control his anger and put it to good use." Bobby held his tongue.

"His name was Adelbert, but everyone called him Bert. Like you, he was small for his age. They called him Red Bert, because he was always enraged. He couldn't get along with his father, a shoemaker. He couldn't get along with the schoolmistress, who happens to be my sister. He couldn't get along with the Lord, the Sheriff, the other boys, or even the girls.

"Except for one girl. He was in love with the sweetest, kindest girl in the village. Her name was (and still is) Frances the Fair. Bert had no idea what to say to a girl. Whenever their paths crossed he turned bright red and muttered angrily to himself: 'Bert's too rough for Missy Frances!' Frances thought Bert hated her, and avoided him.

"Everything changed on the day that a wolf stole Frances's kitten. Frances was a very sensible girl, but the news made her crazy with grief. Word of her misfortune spread through the town. When Bert heard, he went beet red. He called his big dog, Rex, and ran to Frances's cottage. 'Which way did he go? Which way?' This made Frances cry all the harder, but she pointed towards the deepest, darkest part of the forest. Bert and Rex crashed into the underbrush.

"It was starting to get dark. Frances had been worried about her kitten, but now she was worried about Bert. She set off after him, even though she was wearing cloth slippers and a light shift. Bert and Rex plowed onward; Frances ran after the thrashing noise they were making.

"After a while the sounds died out in the wind. Frances turned to go back. But it was almost pitch dark. She was lost. If she wandered any further her footsteps might attract a wolf or a bear.

"She decided to climb a tree. With luck, Bert and Rex would come back that way. She climbed high up in an oak tree and settled down to wait. The woods were very quiet. She couldn't hear Bert and Rex, but she did become aware of sounds at the foot of her tree, something swishing around in the fallen leaves. There was a sharp whine, followed by a bark and a scuffle. She could picture what was going on. Two wolves were fighting over something down there, probably her kitten.

"Finally she heard footsteps and an angry voice: 'Where are you, you stupid kitten?' She held her breath until Bert was fairly close.

"Then she said in an ordinary voice, trying to sound calm, 'Bert, it's Frances. I followed you. Now I'm up in a tree. There are two wolves at the base of my tree.' The wolves started to growl. Bert's dog growled back.

"'Frances!' shouted Bert and ran towards the sound of her voice. Rex went for the she-wolf and locked his teeth on the back of her neck. The two of them swayed and struggled. Bert ran at the he-wolf, which was snarling and baring its teeth. It lunged at Bert's neck. Bert stepped aside. He caught the wolf's tail in passing, gave it a jerk and a twist. The wolf dropped on his back. Bert was so angry, so hot and red, he managed to swing the wolf around by the tail and smash it into a tree. It dropped to the ground, dead. The she-wolf was still grappling with Rex. Bert grabbed her ears. Together, he and Rex forced her to the ground. Bert stomped and punched her till she ran off howling.

"He paused to catch his breath. Then he invited Frances to climb down. He told what had happened with the wolves and offered to guide her home. It was Rex who sniffed out the way. They got home just after dinner, Frances in her shredded slippers, Bert red in the face, dragging a dead wolf. The kitten was gone, but Bert and Frances had found each other.

"They were 13 at the time. At 18 they got married. Frances gradually tamed Bert. She knew his heart was good, and he appreciated that. Because he wanted nothing but happiness for Frances, Bert learned how to make charcoal and is now the best charcoal maker in Beckham Wood. They have three little daughters, two dogs and a vegetable garden. On Sundays they go rowing on the river. Only a few things make Bert see red now, mostly taxes and the weather.

"Anger can be a good thing if it makes you brave. Not if it makes you lash out at people who wish you well."

Bobby wondered whether Bronwen would ever follow *him* into the darkest part of the forest. He thought not. They were coming up to Effling's Farm, so the Vicar bade them farewell.

"Not bad for a vicar," said Fahd. Bobby did not reply. His ankles still hurt.

In the distance a church spire marked the town of Gambrell. The Count of Gambrell was said to be a good ruler. When people told Bobby this, he knew they were criticizing his own behavior. So he disliked the Count.

Chapter VII. Gambrell

They reached the town in mid-afternoon. Gambrell bustled with activity. They strolled along narrow streets, watching leather workers cut and sew, greengrocers wash and trim, laundresses iron, weavers weave, carpenters measure and saw. As evening approached cows were driven in to be milked and sheep to be penned for the night. Farmers tramped in, sweaty and happy to be finished for the day. Fahd and Bobby picked a busy corner and sang their new duet. The townspeople liked it and showered them with coins, plus an apple, some wildflowers and a tightly-folded love note.

The circle of listeners parted respectfully when a tall man in a floppy velvet hat pushed through. He waited for the song to end and said to Fahd, "I couldn't help admiring your music. My Lord the Count loves music. May I invite you to sing at his table tonight? If you need a place to stay we will happily put you up."

Fahd accepted with pleasure, even though Bobby was making faces and shaking his head.

"Come to the fortress after sundown. The Bailiff will be expecting you. I am Hugh, Sheriff of this County." With a tip of his hat he strode off.

"No!" whispered Bobby. "I won't sing for the Count!"

"Yes you will," said Fahd. "It's a great chance for us."

Bobby cursed, but Fahd had started singing again, so no one heard. That evening they walked up to the walls of the fortress. There was a little wooden door cut into one of the gates. A guard peered out. Bobby glared at him.

Fahd stepped between them. "Fahd the musician, looking for the Bailiff." The soldier smiled and let them in. Inside the walls stood the tall castle where the Count and his family lived. The Bailiff led them to an empty stable built into the wall. There was clean straw on the floor. He showed them where to wash and promised to fetch them at dinnertime. Fahd and Bobby rehearsed their duet. Bobby was feeling ornery. He himself was a lord. How could he behave like a servant?

The Bailiff eventually led them up to a banquet room, where the table was set for a dozen or more guests. The wine glasses sparkled with the glow of dozens of candles. There were tapestries on the walls – hunting and harvest scenes.

After awhile the Count strolled in with the Countess, their children and retainers. Their oldest boy was about 13. His hair was prettily curled, his tights were inky black, his tunic was embroidered with gold. He ignored Bobby. The Count looked toward Fahd and Bobby, but didn't seem to see them. Servants ran in with trays of roast meat, grilled fish and vegetables, rolls and breads, sauces and gravies. They kept the wine glasses full and ran back to the kitchen whenever something was wanted.

The Bailiff signaled to Fahd, who struck up a quiet song. No one paid much attention. Then Fahd and Bobby sang their duet in Arabic. A hush fell over the table. At the song's conclusion the Count called them over. "Are you gypsies? Was that your gypsy tongue?"

"It is Arabic, my lord, the language of Tunisia, my home in Africa. It was called Carthage in ancient times." The count had never seen anyone like Fahd. He secretly wished he could meet Fahd's sister.

"And you, my lad," said the Count, speaking to Bobby, "are *you* from Tunisia, with your pale complexion and rosy cheeks?" The Count was chewing a mouthful of venison. The ladies studied Bobby as if he were some interesting kind of goat. The Count's son looked at him with disdain.

"I'm . . . I'm . . ." spluttered Bobby, barely able to speak. "I'm an Englishman like you . . . and just as good!"

The Count's face darkened. Two men at the table pushed back their chairs. Fahd put his hands on Bobby's shoulders.

"Mad!" spat the Count's son.

"That will do, Tristan." The Count wiped his mouth on his sleeve. "Arno!" he said. The Bailiff stepped out of the shadows. "Thrash him." The Count glanced up at Fahd. "Please continue." Then he turned to chat with his neighbor. Fahd strummed on his guitar and tried to remember a song. The Bailiff dragged Bobby away. Tristan grinned.

The Bailiff dragged Bobby outside, to the base of a wall. He barked an order and a soldier ran up with a willow switch. To Bobby he said, "Pull down your pants. I'm going to cane you. I want you to learn from this. I will cane your legs till you say you're sorry." Bobby stood up straighter.

The Bailiff aimed his stick at Bobby's calves and said, "There are two kinds of people: One, Commoners. Two, Nobles." He gave Bobby a stinging blow. "Which are you?"

Bobby was trying not to cry. At the same time he was trying to hold onto his anger. He looked up and answered, "an oyster!" The Bailiff, a heavyset man, scowled. He leaned back, bent his knees and slashed Bobby's legs again.

"Wrong," said the Bailiff. "Try again. You and I are commoners. The Count of Gambrell is a lord. He has purer blood than we do. Who is better, you or the Count?"

Bobby steeled himself and said, "Same difference." The Bailiff threw his weight into a third blow. An "Oof" escaped from between Bobby's gritted teeth.

The Bailiff tried another approach. "When commoners speak to their betters, they do not say, 'Hey!' They say 'If it please you, my Lord.' Now, tell me what you would say to a lord."

"Bedwetter!" said Bobby.

"Smack!" went the Bailiff's cane, which had raised a wet red stripe on the back of Bobby's legs. Bobby's knees buckled, but he didn't cry. He looked the Bailiff in the eye.

The Bailiff's anger was waning. This boy was not going to give in. The Bailiff tried one last lesson. "You are a child. The Count is a grown man. Don't you owe your elders some respect?"

Bobby hesitated. He wasn't sure. Fahd appeared at the bailiff's side, worried and out of breath. "I might," said Bobby grudgingly. The Bailiff permitted himself a little smile and turned to Fahd.

"The two of you will now leave Gambrell. Consider yourselves lucky that this little runt can still walk." Fahd inspected Bobby's bleeding legs. He took Bobby by the hand and led him out the gate.

Bobby could not stand up. He could not sit down. His rage cooled and the wound started to pulse. Finally he allowed himself to sob. Fahd wrapped him in a hug. When Bobby could finally speak, he said, "I won't knuckle under! We're just as good as that Count, if not better!"

Fahd looked thoughtfully at Bobby. "Do you mean *you're* as good, because you're an earl?"

Bobby didn't even have to think. "No. *You* are, because you go through the world making people happy. You earn your own keep and do no harm."

Secretly Fahd agreed, but he feared these ideas were somewhat advanced for the twelfth century. "I am not noble, but I do my best to be good."

"You *are* good," said Bobby. "I want to be like you. Are you a nobleman in your own country?"

"No," said Fahd. "My father raises radishes and weasels."

Chapter VIII. The Shepherdess

The two spent the night in an empty horse stall next to some occupied ones. Bobby couldn't get his legs comfortable. They still stung. In the morning Fahd and Bobby set out again on the high road.

They were coming into a rugged, windswept district. Houses and towns were farther apart. On every side there were broad hillsides, divided into patchworks of fields. Bare rock formations jutted up here and there. The fields were bordered by stone fences, not hedges. The wind blew harder here with fewer trees to slow it down. The road threaded its way between the hills, alongside gurgling streams and wind-raked lakes.

Around midday, when they were starting to think about lunch, they came upon a flock of sheep drinking at a stream. The shepherd was a girl of 17 or so, in a broad straw hat. She had an open face, a lovely smile, and a modest manner. Fahd and Bobby asked if they could join her, and offered to share their lunch. She agreed. Her name was Ennis.

"A fine flock," said Fahd.

"Yes it is," she said. "Next spring they will give us thirty baskets of wool."

Long days in the sun had turned Ennis a golden color. She just about matched Fahd. Her fingernails were broken and there were scars on her ankles. Fahd could picture her in all kinds of weather, protecting the little lambs. "Have you no brothers to tend the flock?" he asked.

"Oh I have brothers all right," laughed Ennis. "But they are too fine to watch sheep."

"That sounds like a story," said Fahd. "May we walk along with you?"

"I'll tell you my story," she said, "as long as you don't pity me. I like sheepherding."

"We like it too," said Fahd.

"We're interested in sheep!" threw in Bobby. Ennis gave them a stern look to discourage flirting. She met plenty of men who thought a pretty shepherdess would be lonely. She wasn't.

"Hi!" she shouted to her sheep, who were drinking from the stream. They looked up obediently, water draining out of the corners of their mouths. They bumped confusedly into each other, waiting to see what came next. "We're going up into the hills," she told Bobby and Fahd. "It's not on your way." They didn't mind. "Then you take the right side, and watch that old ram with the black ears. He likes to wander. Hey! Let's go!"

Looking startled, the sheep clambered up the muddy riverbank and headed uphill. Ennis, Fahd and Bobby walked behind, fanning out to keep the sheep in a bunch.

"I am the youngest of four children," began Ennis, "and the only girl. My father's a farmer. He grows wheat, rye and vegetables above our village. We graze three milk cows and this flock of sheep. We've got a few hens and an herb garden. Our harvests are plentiful and our animals are sound. Because of that there is more work than one man can do. My mother helps out, but my father always wanted a fine crop of sons.

"Rodney was my parents' first child. He is now 26. When he was just a little boy my mother noticed his fine, sweet voice and came to believe he was a musician. Even though my father needed help on the farm, she sent Rodney to the monastery to study. He learned to read music and he learned to read books. The monks taught him to be a monk – study, pray and make jelly. For years he never saw a girl or a featherbed or a Christmas dinner. He hasn't been home for five years. We're told he's a wonderful singer.

"The next child was Frederick. When he was very young, my mother noticed Frederick had a talent for making things. He made toys from scraps of wood and metal. He drew pictures in the dust with a stick. He made up long stories and told them to our dog. My mother came to believe that Frederick should be a master craftsman, making stained glass windows or carving statues for a church. At the age of seven, just when he was starting to become useful on the farm, she apprenticed him to a stone carver working at Sheringham Cathedral. When Frederick finished his apprenticeship at the age of 18, he came to see us. Then he ran away to sea. He didn't want to be a stonecarver. We haven't seen him since.

"When my third brother, Alwyn, was born, Father was determined to make him a farmer. Alwyn turned out to like farm chores. He was always at my father's side, admiring his big, strong hands, his gentle way with the animals, his gift for fixing things. A farmer has to know a little bit of everything – weather, carpentry, animals, medicine, plants. I think my father purposely kept him out late, so Mother couldn't discover some special talent. When I came along, three years after Alwyn, Dad hoped Mother would focus on me.

"It worked out the other way round. Alwyn got sick and had to stay indoors for a few weeks. My mother decided he was delicate. She warned him not to get tired or wet. She told him that sunburn and dirty clothes are the mark of a peasant. When Alwyn turned 16 my mother apprenticed him to a cook.

"Now I'm the only child left at home. I'm strong and hard-working, and I've never shown a hint of talent. My mother hopes I will catch the eye of some fine gentleman and marry above my rank. My father hopes I will marry a young farmer who can help him and eventually take over the farm. Hi! Bellerophon! Not so fast!"

The old ram was heading back downhill. Bobby chased him, but he only speeded up. "Don't run after him," Ennis said. "Run around in front of him." Bobby did, and Bellerophon turned uphill.

"What kind of man are *you* hoping to marry?" asked Fahd.

"I am not hoping to marry anyone," answered Ennis.

Bobby was discouraged by this answer. He had been thinking about revealing he was an earl. But Fahd liked everything about Ennis. He found out the name of her father – William – and the name of their village – Creegan's Hollow.

It was now late afternoon. They had to be going. Before they did, Fahd told Ennis something about himself – that music and medicine were his trades, that he was a wanderer far from home, and that he was not a Christian but a Muslim. Still, his god was the same as hers, and he honored all of her prophets. He added that he'd been raised on a farm and knew all about radishes. Then he sang a song he had just made up.

> When leaves were turning yellow
> And frost was on the grass
> A promising young fellow
> Went looking for a lass.
>
> Not a thin and pale one
> With thin and wispy hair
> A brown and straight and strong one
> Sturdy as a chair.

He came upon a wooly flock
Drinking at a stream.
There, atop a mossy rock
Sat his very dream.

She was not a wilting bloom
Weak and pale and mute.
She was handy as a broom,
Trusty as a boot.

He became afraid, then.
Worry gripped his breast.
How to make this jaunty wren
Settle in his nest?

I must pass through thin and thick.
I must prove my worth.
Before I ask this pretty chick
To flutter down to earth.

Off he went upon his way
To start a finer life,
In hopes that he'd return someday
Fit for such a wife.

"A song with sheep in it! I didn't know there was one," said Ennis pleasantly.

Fahd blushed. "An English folk song, I believe."

"I hope I can hear it again," said Ennis.

"So do I," said Fahd. He and Bobby shook hands with her and departed. At the bottom of the hill, Fahd strained for a last glimpse of her. He and Bobby didn't speak for a long time, lost in thought.

"What are you thinking?" asked Bobby finally.

"I feel I must do a great deed – kill a dragon or stop a plague – to earn the right to marry Ennis. Her father will never accept a beggar, especially not a foreign one."

"Would you settle down and farm?"

"Yes," said Fahd, his hand on his heart. "I'm not really a wanderer. It's just that I haven't found a good place to stop."

"If she married *me* Ennis would be a countess," said Bobby defiantly.

"Do you think she wants to be a countess?"

Bobby grimaced. "No. I guess she'll be better off with you."

Chapter IX. A Great Deed

They headed north. Fahd didn't take them anywhere near Ennis's village, for fear of running into her father, who would see him as a worthless gypsy. At the same time he wanted to do his great deed close enough so that William, the father, would hear about it.

They continued on the High Road to the county seat, Medwick. Fahd didn't sing that evening. He didn't want anyone around there to know he worked as a street performer.

He decided he and Bobby would go to work as farm laborers. That way he could learn how to raise wheat and rye. He went to the market to meet some farmers.

Bobby wanted to help. But he wasn't willing to pull weeds. He went to the church to inquire about indoor jobs. The priest looked him over and wondered whether he'd be reliable. "How old are you?" he inquired.

"Sixteen," said Bobby.

The priest gave him a regretful look. "I'm trying to figure out whether you're truthful."

"Oh, eleven then," Bobby confessed.

"Can you read and write?"

"No."

"Have you taken care of little brothers and sisters? Done housework? Sewing or weaving?"

"No," said Bobby. "But whatever I do, I do well."

"What have you done?"

"I can sing a song in Arabic." And he sang it.

"Do you want to learn a trade? Apprentice yourself to a craftsman?"

"I'd like to learn soldiering."

"That will have to wait. Is there any job you'd be good at?"

"Horses." With the priest's help Bobby got a job at the posthouse. He helped with horses rented by travelers and stagecoach drivers. He slept in the stables in case he was needed at night. He wasn't polite and he wasn't very helpful, but he liked horses and the previous stable boy had been a thief.

Fahd found a job with a farmer named Duffin, who raised wheat and rye on the opposite side of town from Ennis. Duffin had an awkward, blushing daughter named Rowen. When Fahd appeared in their low stone hut, Rowen sighed and fainted. Duffin didn't want her marrying a tramp, so he sent her to live with an aunt and uncle. He was only hiring Fahd until the harvest was in.

Both Bobby and Fahd interrogated all the people they met, trying to think of a Great Deed. "What's your biggest problem?" Fahd would ask. People's biggest worry was the weather. They also believed that their children were lazier than they themselves had been. They worried about taxes and the civil wars. They worried about the diseases of chickens, apples and the human foot. And they worried about Ruthless Rembert.

Ruthless Rembert was a robber. He and his band robbed travelers and lonely farmhouses. When vegetables disappeared from gardens, Rembert's men were blamed. They were also blamed when clothes on clotheslines and the odd chicken or goat disappeared. People remembered Rembert as a boy in Medwick. They remembered most of his men, too. These men had tried to make an honest living. But either they didn't own any farmland, or they hadn't learned a trade, or they were slow learners. So they turned to crime.

In those days there was no such thing as a policeman. A powerful lord, like the Count of Gambrell, could try to put Rembert out of business. But Medwick didn't have a powerful lord. Everyone knew where Rembert's camp was – in a forest at the end of a big lake. It was the only hiding place in that windswept countryside. Nobody went near it. The bandits were loud, rough men who would pick a fight over anything. They cursed a lot, took special delight in terrifying women, and made poor people even poorer. Rembert was the curse of Medwickshire.

On Fahd's day off, the first day of the month, he came to Bobby's stable to compare notes on the Great Deed. "We will put Rembert out of business," declared Fahd. He had met farmers who lost the seeds for spring planting. Rembert had cooked them into porridge and eaten them. Other farmers lost oxen, sheep and cows, which were driven away and barbecued. People had lost everything from combs to butter knives to hair nets.

"Okay, Rembert," agreed Bobby. He had heard about Rembert from travelers at the stable. Their wives and daughters had been pushed, insulted and pinched. They had lost their money, their horses, and some of their favorite articles of clothing. Ruthless Rembert grabbed silk handkerchiefs, feathered hats and anything made of fur.

"We can't beat the robbers by force," said Bobby. "We have to outsmart them."

"Hmm," said Fahd. "What if we organized the local farmers into an army, trained them to fight?" Fahd paused to think this over. "But why would they follow a couple of strangers?"

"What if we catch Rembert, like a rabbit in a trap?" asked Bobby.

"That's what I was wondering," said Fahd. They pondered this idea. "I can see a way to catch him," said Fahd. "But I can't see how to hold him."

"What if we push him toward Gambrell?" asked Bobby. "I'm sure the Count could handle him. The Bailiff is a monster!"

"Hmm," said Fahd, liking the idea. The two of them discussed and reflected, rejected some moves and thought up others. They disagreed on only one point. "I'll be doing this alone," said Fahd. "It's dangerous."

"What if *I* want to do a Great Deed?" objected Bobby. He was thinking of Ennis. But there might be a lovely shepherdess closer to his own age. He would want to show *her* he wasn't a pampered little lord.

"I'll think about it," said Fahd, and returned to Duffin's Farm.

Two weeks later Fahd returned in the middle of the night. He woke Bobby by touching his shoulder. He had worked out a very detailed plan for the Great Deed. And almost in spite of himself, he was asking Bobby to play the role of a pampered little lord. No one would ever suspect the Earl of Acton Waters of being in league with an Arab minstrel.

Bobby whistled and agreed. Fahd slipped back to Duffin's Farm. Fahd returned to the stable each of the next five nights. He and Bobby rehearsed their roles, thought about what could go wrong and what to do if it did.

When their plans were complete, each of them quit his job. One crisp autumn morning the townsmen of Medwick saw Fahd and Bobby head up the high road towards Scotland, apparently gone forever.

Chapter X. Alison in Love

About this time a stranger walked into the village of Acton Waters, head held high. He was a nice-looking young man in a boyish way – a little blonde mustache, carefully wetted-down hair. He was well-dressed, though his clothes did not quite match. He could have been well-to-do, or he could have bought his clothing used.

He was pleasant and appealing but not 100% convincing. He smiled a lot, and never disagreed with anyone until they'd left the room. His name was George. He soon acquired the nickname "Smooth," because he slid through life on a smile and a promise, and no one could pin down who or what he was.

Acton Waters was too small to have an inn. He rented a room from Widow Pondscum. The rent was threepence a week. At the end of the first week, when his rent was due, George told the Widow he was waiting for some money from his brother. He would pay what he owed, plus a bonus penny, before the month was out. He made similar arrangements for his meals, and for the skinny horse he rode around the countryside on Sundays.

Some evenings he got into little gambling games with the men of the town, betting on throws of the dice he had in his pocket. They were lovely ivory dice, and he always seemed to win. That's how he managed to pay the Widow, and eventually the owner of the horse. It's also how he came to be despised by the wives and mothers of Acton Waters, who watched their husbands gamble away their families' savings.

One day Countess Alison appeared in the town with her bodyguard. She commanded the men and boys to bow. George did so along with everyone else. When he looked up he was smiling. She noticed. "What are you smiling about?" she asked. "What's your name?"

"George, Your Utterness," he said, so softly that she had to lean towards him to hear. "At your service, my noble dame."

"Noble dame," she thought to herself with mild satisfaction. "And how could someone like you serve me?"

"Oh magnificent and important one," he purred. "Though I am now reduced to wandering I, too, pump with the blood of kings. I, too, once sat at tables loaded with food, wrote poetry, sang ballads and hosted balls in a huge, very fancy palace."

"What?" said Alison, flattered by this grown man's interest. "I suppose your favorite sport is hunting?"

"Oh no, Your Splendidness!" George had done his homework. "I hate violence. I am far more interested in the arts."

"If you're noble, what are you doing here?" Alison gestured at the town's street, with its steaming signs that a herd of cows had just passed through.

"Oh Fine Madam, I was born Sir George of Long Billings. My estates stretched from the River Billings in the north to the Whistling Mountains in the south, from Slime Meadows in the east to the Lumpy Islands in the west. Oh, Long Billings, home of my youth, how I miss you . . . the castle, the stables, the emerald green lawns!"

The men and boys of Acton Waters started to snicker. Alison silenced them: "What do you, in your dirty undershirts, know of nobility? You live with goats! This man is high quality! Sir George," she declared, "I weep for you!" George bowed again. He caught her eye, and winked. She blushed and scurried home.

At the castle she mentioned that a young nobleman was passing through and that she planned to invite him to lunch. She sent one of her soldiers to town with an invitation:

> To George, Knight Intendant of Long Billings.
> From Alison, Countess of Acton Waters.
> The countess requests your pleasure at lunch.
> Midday tomorrow. Clothing: informal.

She brushed her hair to a golden sheen. Whenever she looked in the mirror she pinched her cheeks to heighten their color. She borrowed her mother's earrings and tucked flowers in her hair.

At the appointed time George presented himself at the castle door. He was wearing his best and cleanest outfit, and had polished his teeth with a greenwood stick. The Jester met him at the door.

"Good day, sir. You must be Sir George. I'm Walter, a harmless fool. Shall I announce you?"

"Please do," said George.

"He's here!" screamed the Jester, and ran off. Alison ushered George into the dining room. Her mother was the only other guest. Alison had ordered her father to go and count the clouds. She feared he was too rough around the edges for a refined person like George.

They sat down. George tied a napkin around his neck. In those days people ate with their fingers. George's fingernails were alarmingly black. He chewed so hard that juice squirted out of the corners of his mouth. He belched. He picked his teeth with a chicken bone. Alison decided he must be a simple, honest man.

"I understand you are a knight and heir to a considerable property," said Alison's mother politely. "How do you come to be here?"

George had to wait until he'd chewed the watercress croquettes he'd thrust into his mouth. "My brother," he said. "My evil younger brother took the sceptre and drove me from my domain."

"Have you friends who could help you regain power?" asked Lady Nelda.

"Yes," said George. "Well, no," he added, thinking better of his answer. "My brother employs hundreds of ruffians. He has threatened to cut off my ears."

Alison sighed. George thrust a stuffed green pepper into his mouth.

A light came into his eyes. He shifted the huge wad of food into one cheek. He said with difficulty, "Lady Alishun is the handshomesht young filly in thish and all the shurrounding country. Shinsherely!." He beamed, teeth speckled with green pepper bits. Alison smiled too. She felt he understood her.

"What?" said Alison's mother.

"Alishun is a prime peesh of horshflesh, Lady Waterzh."

Alison whinnied and looked happily into her lap. George was not a polished man. He needed her to smooth out the rough places.

Alison's mother wasn't sure she liked George. When she learned the young man's nickname – "Smooth"– she decided to check his story. She sent her husband off to the south to look for Long Billings.

In the meantime George became a daily visitor at the castle. He studied Alison's mother until his table manners were just about the same as hers. He avoided meat and stuck to boiled greens and roots. Whenever he was alone with Alison he held and kissed her and asked her to marry him. She did not answer right away. She was still just a girl. But she felt that George had the charm and innocence of a little boy.

Two months went by without word from her father. Finally they learned from a traveling friar that he had stopped at the next town. As soon as he got there he ordered a roast beef dinner. The next morning he went fishing. He decided to stay. He joined an order of fisherman friars, men who prayed, studied and worked as fishing guides.

"He is now a holy man," reported the friar. "He has dedicated his life to fishing."

Once he heard that, George made his stories about Long Billings even more extravagant. His castle grew big enough to include a greenhouse and a zoo. His property now stretched across three counties. Before long he asked for Alison's hand in marriage.

Lady Nelda guessed that George, with all his faults, would be an improvement over Alison as the boss of Acton Waters. He might put the Masters back to work. He might bring back meat. He might leave the men and boys alone.

Lady Nelda consented. So did Alison. Lady Nelda explained to George that marrying Alison would not make him the ruler of Acton Waters. Alison would still be that. And if Bobby ever came back he would be the ruler. George didn't particularly mind, since his main goal was a reliable supply of food.

None of George's relatives came to the wedding. He blamed this on the family feud. A toothless old woman did show up claiming to be George's mother. George kicked her and she left. Alison's mother paid for everything, including a few little debts that George had run up in the village.

Alison was deliriously happy. She wore a beautiful white dress. She invited a dozen villagers to witness the wedding and had them hum a tune as she marched down the aisle. She arranged for each of them to be given a glass of beer and a basket of mushrooms.

But her happiness did not last. George put meat back on the menu. He especially like pig's knuckles and cow's tongue – favorites back at Long Billings. The Master of the Hounds taught George how to hunt. Before long he was hunting every day, except when it rained. The Masters were glad to be back at work.

George put a stop to Alison's tours of the village. The villagers were very grateful. But Alison felt that something was off. George stopped calling her "ickle Allie" and "sticky-sweet." He barely noticed her. He ate meat, picked his teeth, wiped his nose with his napkin and burped after every third bite. She wondered whether she had made a mistake. This suited him fine. He was tired of pretending to love her.

She ordered the Master of the Horse to lock up his horse. The Master didn't say no, but he didn't obey, either. She ordered the Master of the Hounds to take away George's weapons. He nodded and bowed, but didn't do it. She ordered the Cook to throw George's freshly-killed meat to the dogs. The Cook only said helplessly: "But my Lady . . ."

"Won't anyone obey me?" shrieked Alison. "Is it because I'm a woman?" In those days marriage was for life. The Catholic Church did not permit divorce.

She called in the Master of the Purse, who needed Alison's signature on checks and documents. He, at least, obeyed her. So Alison finally got her way. She stopped spending money. She fired the orchestra and all but one of the kitchen staff. When George ran out of arrows, Alison clicked her tongue and said, "Can't afford any." The castle started leaking; she wouldn't pay for repairs. The horses went hungry. The cook's budget barely covered salt and onions. The proud castle of Acton Waters became a prison.

Chapter XI. Rembert the Ruthless

When we last saw Fahd and Bobby they were trudging north from Medwick. They walked to the next town, where Fahd did some singing to earn money. He used it to buy supplies for the Great Deed. He took Bobby to a tailor and ordered a fancy suit of pale brown velvet, with puckered sleeves, a pleated shirt and dark green leggings. At other shops they added soft leather boots, a feathered hat and an ebony walking stick.

They went to a humbler tailor, a woman who worked in her own cottage, for a hooded brown monk's robe, a girl's dress and a hooded cape. They explained that the outfits were Hallowe'en costumes. Once they were finished Fahd sewed them into a watertight goatskin. He threw it over his shoulder, tucked a blanket under his arm and headed back to Medwick.

"Good-bye, Bobby," he said to his friend. "I'll see you in a week. If all goes well we'll do a Great Deed. If it doesn't . . . well, you've been a faithful friend. Thank you."

Bobby blinked, gripped Fahd's hand, and bade him farewell. Bobby's part would not begin for another week.

At the edge of town Fahd gave his respectable clothes to a beggar and put on the beggar's fluttering rags. The beggar was happy with the deal. Many of his fleas and bedbugs went off with Fahd.

Fahd skirted Medwick Town and headed for Rembert's secret grove. Once he got to the big lake he stuffed his goatskin into a rotting stump and covered it with leaves. Then he emerged into the sunlight and crunched along the pebbly shore of the lake. He peered warily into the trees. He knew that Rembert's guards were lurking just out of sight.

"Zeep!" An arrow whizzed past his ear. A man with a bow stepped out of the bushes, a huge man with a scar across one cheek, dressed in a bedraggled ball gown of lavender silk.

"Hello, Mr. Dust Mop!" he said with a scowl. "Where do you think you're going?" He reached for another arrow and notched it onto his bowstring.

Fahd didn't have to simulate fear. He was trembling. "Sir . . . I am looking for a friend who lives nearby."

"And who might that be?"

"Wiggin, sir. A shepherd. Wiggin."

"There's no Wiggin here. Bugger off!"

"Are you the sheriff, sir, or a sheriff's man?" asked Fahd in a quavering voice.

"The sheriff's man? Are you daft? I'm Rembert's man – Rembert the Ruthless. An outlaw!" He leaned down and grimaced at Fahd.

Fahd let out his breath. "Whew! It's Rembert I want. I didn't know where to look."

The man put one end of his bow on the ground, leaned on it, and quizzed Fahd. Why did he want to see Rembert? Who was he? What gave him the idea that Rembert was a nice man? Fahd's answers seemed to satisfy him. Finally he grabbed Fahd's blanket roll and spilled the contents on the ground: a guitar, some rags, and a cheese rind.

He nodded towards the guitar. "Can you play this?"

Fahd nodded. "I sing, too."

"We'll see," said the man. With a whistle he summoned another guard to take his place. Then he led Fahd through the woods, following a stream. After 20 minutes they came to a clearing. The open meadow was filled with tethered horses, broken-down carts and carriages and little circles of men play-ing cards. There were easily a hundred men scattered around the clearing. They were rough-hewn types whose language would have shocked their own mothers. They paid no atten-tion to Fahd.

At one end of the meadow was a rocky cliff with a line of trees along the bottom. As they got closer, Fahd saw the mouth of a cave in the shade of an especially big tree. At the mouth of the cave sat a beautiful gypsy woman and a blonde man with a pock-marked complexion. He appeared to be dreaming. He was wearing orange tights, no shirt, a fur coat and a broad-brimmed hat with nodding white plumes. His arms were thick as tree trunks.

He cleared his throat. "Who's this, Rock?"

"He wants to join the band."

"A little puny, ain't he?" The man in the hat looked Fahd up and down. "What's your name, Chicken Ribs?"

"Fahd, your Excellency. I am a musician, a healer and for-tuneteller. I'm not good at fighting, but my other skills might serve you well."

There was a long pause while the man squinted at Fahd. He turned toward the woman. "What do you think, Florizel?"

"Sing something pretty," she said. Fahd sang "Greensleeves." The card players all across the meadow turned to listen. When Fahd strummed the last few notes they burst out cheering.

"Brilliant!"

"Well done, my stoat!" And comments of that kind.

Rembert was mean, but he wasn't a suspicious person. Anyone could join his band. The men liked Fahd's singing, so Rembert let him in. He and his men were bored most of the time.

"What's your name again?"

"Fahd."

"What kind of name is that?"

"Tunisian."

Rembert turned to Florizel. "A gypsy?" She shook her head.

"I come from a great Caliphate that stretches from Mesopotamia all the way to Spain," explained Fahd.

"Yeah, but your name is weird. How 'bout Freddy?" He shouted out across the meadow, "This is Freddy! He's with us now!"

The men cheered again, "Hey, Freddy! Sing 'Froggy Went a'Courting!'"

"Sing 'A Mother's Lament!'" And so on.

"I'm Rembert," said the arch criminal. "You've probably heard my name. The very sound of it curdles the milk in mothers' breasts. If you don't have a blanket we'll find one for you. Sleep wherever you want."

Florizel prompted him: "Come back and sing again."

"Oh yeah," Rembert caught on. "Report to this cave after supper. We want more music." Florizel gave a thumbs up. "Now go find Shorty. He'll be your mother." He returned to his meditation, staring intently up into the trees. Florizel crossed her arms and stared up too.

Rock, Fahd's guide, took him to meet his mother. Shorty turned out to be a tall, bald man in a leather vest. He was making a fire in a circle of rocks. There were about ten fire pits scattered around the meadow. At each one a "mother" was carefully building a fire for the night's meal.

"You want a blanket?" asked Shorty. Fahd indicated that he already had one. "You want a bowl, a cup and a spoon?" Fahd nodded. "You want a lady's maid, a pet wabbit and a peck of strawberries?" Fahd shook his head. "Awright. The cup and bowl and spoon cost money. How much do you have?" Fahd smiled apologetically and held out empty hands. Shorty spat on the ground.

"You can earn some. We go robbing at moonrise!" He reached into a filthy sack and dug out a spoon, a battered metal cup and bowl. Then he made one more observation: "Fight for a sleeping place near the fire. Or you can sleep in the woods with the babies."

Fahd headed into the woods. He wedged his blanket and eating equipment into the fork of a tree. Then he strolled around the camp. A few of the men were napping under the wagons that were drawn up around each fire pit – their only shelter from sun and rain. The horses were tethered to stakes. They looked thin. There were leather chests and saddlebags perched here and there, apparently filled with booty. The camp had the overall look of a junkyard. The ground was littered with chicken bones and other garbage, discarded articles of clothing and broken tools. There were plentiful signs that the meadow got muddy after a rain.

A few of the men looked up as Fahd passed. They gave him either an encouraging smile, an appraising look or a menacing scowl.

"Who's your muvver?" asked one.

"Shorty," answered Fahd.

"Shorty will train you proper," said the man, flashing a whiskery grin.

"Where'd you learn music, mate?" asked another.

"Tunisia," answered Fahd. "That's where I'm from."

"That down Brighton way?" asked the man, scratching his ear.

"Sort of," answered Fahd.

When evening came the clearing filled with the smell of wood smoke and oatmeal. Fahd went to reclaim his bowl and spoon. They were gone. He reported this to Shorty, whose family was seated around the fire, waiting for dinner.

"This is a robber camp! You can't just leave things lying out!" One of the men by the fire broke into a mischievous grin. Shorty addressed him. "You the culprit, Iron Butt?" The man held up Fahd's things and giggled.

When Fahd went over for them, Iron Butt pulled them back. Then he gave them to Fahd. Then he grabbed them back, all the while chattering: "I gave my love a chicken wing and wrapped it in a hornet's sting." Finally he let Fahd keep them, kissed his fingers, and slapped his cheek. The experience reminded Fahd of nursery school. Many of the men seemed like overgrown children – noisy, impulsive and dimwitted.

Porridge was the only thing on the menu that night, plus water dipped from a bucket. On good days there were also scraps of meat or a sliver of pie.

After dinner Fahd reported back to Rembert. The whole camp listened to his songs and cheered. When Rembert's campfire died down and Florizel yawned for the third time, Rembert asked Fahd a little about himself.

"Where you from, Freddy?"

"Gambrell, my Lord."

"You can call me The Ruthless."

"Gambrell, The Ruthless. I used to sing at the Count's table."

"Oh yeah?" Rembert was impressed. "How did you become a penniless wanderer?"

"His Lordship got tired of me," said Fahd.

"Come on, what really happened? You sing like a bird in a tree!"

Fahd shrugged sadly. "The Lord's wife fell in love with me."

"A little monkey like you? What do you think, Florizel?"

She glanced up briefly from her nails, which she was buffing. "Naah! Well, maybe."

"So what did the Lord do?"

"He banished me."

"And what did he do to his wife?"

"Gave her a white horse. To win her back."

"You don't say! I thought he was wise and just. If I was him I would have sent her back to her Mum." He gave Florizel a playful look. She didn't notice.

"What about this Count, Freddy? Is he wise and just? Or not?"

"He's overrated, Ruthless. Everyone says he's wise and just. I say he's a limp rag."

"Well whaddya know? Wishy-washy!"

"I could tell you a million stories . . . all the things I've seen. But the strangest one was the story of the Gallant Halberdier. I don't have time to tell it now, because the moon is rising and I have to go robbing. I could tell it tomorrow night."

"I'd like that, Freddy," said Rembert. "Would you, Flo?"

Florizel said with a yawn, "I guess so. I'm not that interested."

Chapter XII. The Gallant Halberdier

Fahd wandered back to Shorty's campfire. Shorty was surprised to learn that Fahd didn't own a weapon. He reached into his sack and gave Fahd a brick.

"We have highway duty tonight. Your job is to bash whoever we catch."

"Bash?"

"You know, drop the brick. Raise an egg. Geez, where did you grow up – under a cabbage?"

They marched single file to the highway. Then they hid in the bushes. Most of them went to sleep. One or two kept a lookout. After about two hours the lookouts heard the clip clop of hooves and the creaking of wooden wheels. They made clicking noises with their tongues. The other bandits woke up and drew their weapons.

When the cart reached their hiding place they jumped out and surrounded it. The horse was so old and tired it simply stopped. It didn't whinny or rear up or shift nervously in its traces.

"We're Rembert's men," announced Shorty. "Give us your money and your fine clothing." The man in the cart simply sat there.

"It's Jake," he said dryly. "You already took everything."

"We'll take the horse," said Shorty, grabbing its halter.

"The horse is so worn out he probably won't live through the night," said Jake.

"We'll eat it," said Shorty. Jake got down from his seat and started to unharness the horse.

"Oh, never mind," said Shorty. Jake climbed back onto the wagon and slapped the horse's back with his reins. It didn't move.

Shorty kicked it. "You're wasting our time, Dobbin!"

The horse staggered into motion. "Thanks, Shorty," said Jake. The robbers returned to the bushes.

The next traveler, on foot, was so quiet the watchers almost missed him. By the time someone whistled he was past their hiding place. They chased him down.

"We're Rembert's men," recited Shorty. "Give us your money and your fine clothing!"

"Oh Sir," cried the traveler, "Don't hurt me!"

"Freddy!" called Shorty. "Hurt him." Fahd banged the man lightly on the top of the head with his brick. "Harder!" said Shorty.

"Harder yourself," said the man, and kicked Shorty in the soft area between the legs. Then he sprinted off into the darkness.

"Get him!" Shorty ordered. But the men just stood there.

After awhile one of them said, "We'll never catch him now, Boss." They went back into the bushes. All except Shorty, who was crumpled up by the side of the road.

When the sky started to lighten they still hadn't managed to steal anything. Shorty told them they weren't going home until they did. Finally, just as steam was starting to rise from the grass, a fat horse came riding along. The rider, a middle-aged man, looked well-fed. Half of the men sprang out behind him. Half of them sprang out ahead. The man had no choice but to stop.

"Get off your horse," screeched Shorty. "Baptize him, Fred!" Fahd tapped the man's head with his brick. To everyone's delight, the man burst into tears. He took off his fine clothes and left them in the road, reached into his saddlebag and handed the men a leather pouch full of gold coins. Then he wandered off into the fields in his underwear, sobbing.

"What's wrong with him?" asked Shorty. "Maybe you banged him too hard." Fahd shrugged. Mounting the horse, Shorty led his little band back into the woods. They presented their loot to Rembert, who awarded one gold coin to Shorty.

"Good job, Freddy," said Shorty. "You can keep the cup and spoon." He laid down next to the campfire and went to sleep. Fahd made a bed of leaves in the woods. That night after supper he presented himself at Rembert's cave.

"Tell us more about the Count of Gambrell," urged Rembert.

"I will," said Fahd, and proceeded to tell this tale.

"When I was court musician, I used to play and sing every evening in the dining room. I would also entertain at picnics, birthday parties, and weddings. When the Countess had a headache, I would sing her to sleep. I gave music lessons to the children. When I wasn't singing, I was hanging around waiting to sing. So I overheard a lot of conversation and got to know all the visitors to the fortress.

"One visitor made a particular impression on me – the one I call the Gallant Halberdier. He was a soldier – a big, broad-shouldered guy. He was always on the lookout, never relaxed. He was on his way home from the Crusades. Naturally, people wanted to hear about his experiences.

"He stayed for several nights, and each night at dinner he would tell stories. I heard all of them, because no one called for music as long as he was there. He told about the endless journey to the East, the hunger and sickness, the sieges and battles and the final conquest of Jerusalem. Although he was the third son of a count, with no hope of inheriting his father's lands, he became a count in the Holy Land. King Godfrey of

Jerusalem made him Count of Jericho, the owner of a city on the River Jordan.

"To guard the city he recruited soldiers among the men who had washed up in the Holy Land – Crusaders, beaten enemies, landless peasants. He brought three of them to England – an African, an Arab and a Frenchman. They were a striking sight when they clattered into the courtyard. First came the Halbardier on a tall warhorse, wearing shiny armor and carrying a halberd – a lance with an axe blade on one side. Then came the African on a light, prancing Arabian stallion, followed by a horse-drawn cart with a soldier on each side. The cart carried nothing but an iron-bound chest.

"The Halberdier's soldiers slept with the servants and soldiers of the Fortress of Gambrell, including me. I hit it off immediately with the Arab. We speak the same language and worship the same prophet. The soldier's name was Hassan. He came from a village near Jericho. He followed the Halberdier to seek his fortune. But he was finding England very cold. The food was too bland and the houses too damp. I told him my own story; we talked a lot.

"Everyone wondered what was in the chest. What had the Halberdier brought back? Hassan told me all he knew. The chest was very heavy. Every night, no matter where they were, they had to lug it into the Halberdier's chamber, next to his bed. The Halberdier promised his men a rich reward if they got it safely home. At an inn in Romania two men tried to steal it. The Halberdier killed them. Then he roused his soldiers in the night and they hurried toward the Austrian border.

"It was rumored in Jericho that the Halberdier had found a great treasure in Jerusalem. When the Crusaders swarmed over the walls, wealthy Muslim families locked themselves into their houses. Crusaders smashed down the doors and barged in. It was said that the Halberdier stumbled into the home of Jerusalem's ruler. If so, he would have found a lot of gold, a lot of jewels and fine things. No one knew for sure. It was possible, on the other hand, that his chest contained a holy relic – a splinter of the True Cross, a tooth from one of Christ's disciples, or a bottle with the dried blood of a saint. It might also have contained nothing more valuable than a cask of water from the River Jordan, holy water to be used in masses and baptisms.

"After three days at Gambrell the Halberdier was impatient to be on his way. He set out with his men on a rainy morning. The Count served them a hearty breakfast of scrambled eggs and toast, kissed the Halberdier on both cheeks and saw him out. Within a half an hour he gathered twenty of his own men in the courtyard, all fully armed, and rode out. What their mission was, none of them has ever said. He swore them to secrecy. I've always wondered what was in that chest, but I'll never know." Fahd prepared to leave.

Rembert raised a hand. "You can't stop now! What happened next?" Even Florizel seemed curious.

"If you wish, I'll tell you all I know tomorrow night." Fahd stepped out of the circle of light and melted into the night.

Chapter XIII. The Mystery of the Ironbound Chest

The next night was a Thursday, the night of the week when Rembert's own family went out to rob. But contrary to all custom, he stayed home. Even before it got dark, as he and Florizel ate their porridge, he ordered Fahd to tell the rest of the story. When Fahd arrived at the cave door they were discussing the Halberdier, the chest and the Count's armed band.

Fahd picked up the thread. "The Count and his men galloped out of the gate. They returned within an hour at a walking pace. They brought nothing and no one back. They dismounted, stabled their horses, and returned to their everyday lives. It was possible, though no one could say for sure, that there were a few spatters of blood on their clothing and their horses' skirts. They might have been hunting for boars. They might have chanced upon a wolf. No one knows.

"Life returned to normal except for one thing. That night the Countess came to dinner with a new ring. It was gold, with a giant amber-colored stone. Everyone at dinner praised it. Someone swore it must be a sapphire from the East. The Count said it was just a garnet, a common stone from Bohemia, sold in all the cathedral towns."

Here Rembert exclaimed, "They robbed the Halberdier!"

Fahd shook his head. "They returned empty-handed."

"They hid it in the woods!"

Fahd frowned. "The Count is no fighter. He could never pull off a robbery."

"Rembert!" piped in Florizel. "A big sapphire!" Rembert silenced her with a look.

"If the Count robbed them," wondered Fahd, "why didn't the Halberdier come to get it back? He looked like a pretty tough guy."

Rembert smiled mysteriously. He knew, but he didn't expect a simpleton like Fahd to guess the truth. He did ask this: "And what precious things appeared after that?"

Fahd looked thoughtful. "There were a few more things . . . a gold chalice in the chapel, a circlet of black river pearls, a diamond tiara. The Count said he bought them at the Midsummer Fair in Durham. He saved them to surprise his wife as the year went on.

Rembert asked no further questions about the Halberdier. But he questioned Fahd about the Fortress of Gambrell – how many soldiers, how wide the moat, how tall the walls. Fahd answered patiently, adding, "If you wish to rob the Count, I am your man. He punished me for his wife's misplaced passion. She loved me because her husband is so wishy-washy."

During the next few days Fahd overheard a lot of chatter about Gambrell. Rembert was asking around for advice and information. Who was from the town? Who knew someone there? Who knew someone in the castle? Fahd continued to sing in the evening and continued to do his job as Shorty's basher.

The next robbing trip was to a farm. Fahd took care not to be seen by the farmer in case it was Ennis's father. He picked out a fat sheep and drove it back to Rembert's camp. At daybreak, as he settled down to sleep, a commotion aroused him.

Another raiding party was returning. They were greeted by shouts and laughter.

"Lord Egg Cup!"

"Peep peep, Chick!"

"Straighten your wig!"

Fahd ran to see what was happening. Bruise, one of the den mothers, was driving a young captive through the camp with an ebony walking stick. The boy was terrified, stumbling ahead with his eyes on the ground. He wore beautifully tailored clothes, now untucked. Bruise took him to Rembert, who emerged from the cave in a silken dressing gown and matching head scarf.

"Who's this, Bruise? We don't take captives!"

Bruise smiled. "Ask him."

"Who are you, little peacock?"

The boy looked up and shivered. He whispered something. Rembert grabbed his collar and shook him. "Speak up!"

"Earl of Acton Waters." It was Bobby.

"Well, I'll be," said Rembert.

Florizel appeared, rubbing her eyes. She was wrapped in a stiff Turkish rug. She curtsied as well as the stiff carpet permitted. "Howdeedo, Lord Blinky," she said. "Wet our pants, did we?" She gave a trilling, musical laugh.

"Ask him where he's been," smirked Bruise.

"Where?" demanded Rembert. Bobby cleared his throat and swallowed, but he couldn't produce a sound. Rembert put his ear next to Bobby's mouth and punched his side. Bobby squeaked.

Finally he croaked out, "Gambrell." There were smiles all around.

"Gambrell, is it?" Rembert bowed deeply. "A visit to the Count? Stag hunt? Country dancing?"

Florizel threw in, "Strawberries and clotted cream? Larks' tongues?" And giggled.

Looking down, Bobby murmured, "Something like that, yes."

Rembert clapped Bobby on the shoulder. "I'd like to introduce myself, Your Earlship. I'm Rembert. The Ruthless. I'm famous for my Sunday dinners – I roast little fellows like you on a spit, with chestnuts and fresh vegetables and two fat fowls, one at your head, one at your feet, for drippings. Mind you, I do not eat friends. Are you my friend?" Bobby nodded. "That's all right, then."

Rembert gestured Bruise to take Bobby away. Catching sight of Fahd in the crowd, Rembert summoned him over.

"Do you know him?"

Fahd shook his head. "I've heard of him. But I never saw him at Gambrell."

"We'll soon find out what he knows," said Rembert with a sly look.

The next morning Bobby was brought to Rembert's campfire. By this time his fine clothes were gone, stripped off by the robbers. He was wearing a pair of loose canvas trousers held up by rope suspenders, a fluffy pink sweater and mismatched socks. Rembert had stationed Fahd some distance behind Bobby in the circle of onlookers.

"Gambrell . . . Are you friends with the Count, Earl?"

"He is my kinsman, yes." Rembert glanced over at Fahd for confirmation. Fahd gave a tiny nod.

"And your visit. Long?"

Bobby was trying to recover his noble bearing. "I went to Gambrell to help the Count collect his rents. He will return the favor next month, coming to Acton Waters to help me with mine."

"Is that hard, collecting rents?"

"Oh no, we just take what we're owed – crops, animals and so forth. If the farmers try to hold out we use a little muscle."

"Ah," said Rembert, "sounds just like robbing. How long does it take?"

"I was in Gambrell for a little over two weeks. I don't see how this concerns you, Sir." Bobby adopted a lordly tone. Rembert encouraged him.

"It concerns me not, my Lord." Florizel cackled from somewhere within the cave. "But one thing I do wonder about. Draw me a picture of the noble life. A person such as I can only dream about it. We *are* friends?" Bobby gave a solemn nod. "Do they have many serving men in Gambrell? Many armed retainers? Only a few, I suppose?"

Bobby laughed at Rembert's ignorance. "You are mistaken, Sir. The Count of Gambrell has at least 35 household servants, 20 gardeners and 50 armed men. His style of life is rather grand."

"And his defensive works? Formidable?" inquired Rembert with raised eyebrows. "Begging your pardon, but I am a serious student of fortification."

Bobby now hit his stride. "The Fortress of Gambrell has stone ramparts 30 feet high and 12 feet wide. The moat is a good 30 feet across and deeper than a tall horse. Only a force with siege engines and a great deal of patience could ever hope to get inside."

"And once inside, my Lord?" asked Rembert. "More lines of defense?"

"I think not," said Bobby severely. "No army will ever get past those walls."

Rembert narrowed his eyes. "No archers' slots facing into the court? The castle has no high windows, no armored doors? If an enemy got past the walls, the Count would be at his mercy?"

"Sir," said Bobby haughtily. "No enemy ever will. The Count's home is perfectly safe. It is an airy, bright pavilion, not a jail."

Rembert raised his eyebrows quizzically in Fahd's direction. Fahd gave a confirming nod. Rembert leaned his chin thoughtfully on a fist. "Sounds like a lovely place, Lord Waters."

From inside the cave Florizel agreed, "Posh!"

Rembert continued. "The general mode of life is top class? Roast goose and cracklings? Fine dinnerware and linens?"

Bobby raised his eyebrows. "The Count is . . . well fixed." Rembert waited to hear more. "A poor lord like me, who eats more or less what his cows eat, when he looks around, it's like a dream." Rembert grinned slyly, but made no comment. "The Countess wears a sapphire as big as a thrush egg! The communion chalice is heavy gold! One evening the Count pulled me aside and showed me . . . " Bobby stopped and shook his head.

Florizel now joined the circle by the fire. "Showed you something? Something rich and rare?"

A cloud passed over Bobby's face. "I . . . well . . . the Count took me aside and told me an improper joke. I could not repeat it to a lady."

Rembert looked into Bobby's eyes. "I don't understand, my Lord. Are you hiding something from us? Friends don't have secrets from each other." Rembert looked around at his men. The men seemed to agree. Bruise stepped forward and punched Bobby in the eye.

"None of that, now, Bruise! The Earl is our good little friend!" warned Rembert.

Bruise then pinched Bobby's nose so hard his fingers left angry marks. In spite of his best efforts, Bobby began to cry.

Rembert put his face right up to Bobby's. "You were saying, Earl, that the Count pulled you aside and showed you something."

Bobby squared his shoulders. "I gave my word as a gentleman I would never tell."

"Are you a gentleman?" roared Rembert. "I don't think so! Cut off his fingers, starting with the pinkies!" Rembert turned and stalked into the cave. Florizel stayed by the fire with Bobby.

The robbers tied Bobby's hands. He sobbed. His nose ran. The men threw him down and tied his legs. Then they hoisted him up like a sack of wheat. Florizel leaned over him, letting her warm breath play over his face. "Couldn't you tell *me* what you saw, my fine fellow?" she whispered. "I will never tell anyone else."

"Yes!" groaned Bobby. Florizel raised a hand. The men paused. Mustering a last shred of pride, Bobby said, "You. Not these men." Florizel put her ear next to Bobby's mouth. He whispered a few sentences.

"I will carry this secret to the grave," she said, winking at the men. "Rembert!" Rembert came to the edge of the shadows. "The Earl told me his secret. Can he keep his fingers?"

Rembert shrugged and went back into the cave. From someplace far within he said, "Oh, do whatever you like."

"Let him go," she said to the men. "Give him some porridge." To Bobby she said sweetly, "We mean you no harm, Earl. The boys was just having some fun."

Bobby was untied. As soon as he could stand up they marched him away. Florizel told Rembert what Bobby had whispered – just what Rembert had imagined. Bobby had also told Florizel where to look – in the Count's chapel, in a stone casket with the sculpture of a knight lying on the lid, a knight named Sir Balsam.

Chapter XIV. The Plan Takes Shape

Rembert sent scouts to Gambrell. They checked the height of the walls, the width and depth of the moat. Chatting with the townspeople, they confirmed that the Count had fifty soldiers. None of the townsmen had ever been through the gates. They had mixed opinions about the layout inside the walls. Bobby and Fahd were still Rembert's best sources.

The walls were surrounded by a moat. Getting over the walls would take some ingenuity. There was no dry land to rest a ladder on. On the plus side, the Count would not be expecting them. No one had ever attacked the Fortress of Gambrell. The moat had not been deepened since it was built, hundreds of years before. In places it was almost filled with silt and fallen leaves.

The town square stood next to the Fortress. On market days it was packed with rows and rows of stalls. After a market some of the vendors would bed down for the night there. They slept under their carts and left in the morning. In the evening they would gather round campfires, sing and tell stories. This could be a good cover for Rembert's band.

Armed with his scouts' reports, Rembert held strategy meetings. Fahd was included. After the second meeting Fahd surprised Rembert by asking for a moment of private conversation.

"Ruthless," he said with an apologetic shrug, "no one desires the success of your operation more than myself. The

Count is a vicious, no-good man. But after prayerful reflection, I have decided to ask your permission to stay home."

"What? Not go to Gambrell? Shorty says you're almost as cruel as him!"

"I hope so, Ruthless. But there's a lady involved here, the Countess. We had . . . a little thing going. I don't want her to blame me for this. And I beg you to treat her gently. If you grant my wish I will not ask for a share of the loot. I just want the Count to pay. That will be reward enough."

Rembert snorted. He could see Fahd's point. He didn't want Florizel hearing about some of the things he'd done.

Fahd went on. "Someone will have to stay here to protect Florizel. Also we'll have to guard the Earl, so he doesn't run squealing to the Count. I'll stay in the cave with Florizel and the Earl."

Rembert thought it over. In the end he consented. Given Fahd's delicate feelings toward the Countess, he would be a good protector for Florizel. And someone had to keep an eye on the little Earl.

Bobby still belonged to Bruise. Bruise was a stocky man in a dirty workmen's blouse. He had a square, clean-shaven jaw and straight yellow hair chopped at ear level. When speaking he gave glimpses of gray and yellow teeth.

To harden the little Earl up, Bruise gave him training exercises, such as jumping back and forth over a log a thousand times. Another exercise was trying to catch hot porridge in spoonfuls flipped toward your open mouth. Most of it lands on your clothes or on other parts of your face. You are allowed to scrape it off and eat it.

XV. The Story of Bruise

In hopes of befriending Bruise, Bobby asked him how he'd become a bandit. Bruise wasn't shy about explaining; nobody had ever asked him before. He was the ninth of eleven children. His father had been a candlemaker. By the time Bruise was born his father was an old man. He died when Bruise was five, leaving his family nothing but a pot of grease.

Bruise's mother, with one baby at her breast and another on her hip, tried selling baked goods. When that failed she tried selling dried flowers. When that failed she sold roots, berries and birds' eggs gathered in the wood. When that failed she sold three of the children – the ones who were ten, eleven and thirteen. Two were bought by farmers. The third was bought by a harness maker. They didn't mind being sold, because for over a year the family had been eating nothing but roots and berries.

Bobby had never been a very good listener. But this story was beginning to touch even *his* little heart.

"I helped my mother scour the woods," said Bruise. "But I wasn't much help, because I ate almost everything I found. We would scatter through the woods and get lost. Little Peeper would wander down into a creek bed. Fan would climb a hill and disappear down the other side. Bunty would fall asleep under a tree. At the end of the day my mother would call us. She would gather us up, one by one, until we were all holding hands in a long line.

"The woods were not very big. On every side you could look down on farmland – cozy cottages with chickens and milk cows. Looking at them, we would dream of milk and sausages. We would dream of having a Dad to tell us stories. We would dream of having a dog. We would dream of being warm at night.

"We used to fight over the littlest of things. That's how I got the name Bruise (my real name is Harold). We would fight over a dead ladybug. We would fight over an acorn. I learned the secret of winning: only fight someone smaller than you. Then go crazy. Just hit and bite and claw and squeeze until the other person gives up. If you are hurt, fight harder. If you are broken, fight harder. When the other person sees how crazy you are, he will fear you. And that will help you win.

"Winter was the hardest time for us. When snow covered the ground we began to starve. The first time my sister Lacy stole a chicken egg, my mother beat her. So the next time she stole an egg Lacy kept it for herself. We other children also began to steal. In barns we would find cured hams, grain, even apples and pears. In gardens we would dig up beets and onions and carrots. We became liars. We told our mother that some-one gave us a ham, or that we had found dried fruit lying on the ground. Sometimes we didn't bring our booty home, or only shared it with another brother or sister. As soon as my sisters got old enough to bear children they married any lout who would have them.

"The farmers began to keep an eye on our family. When they saw us in the town they gave us angry looks. Then a farmer caught Rolf redhanded with a baby pig. They took Rolf to the squire. The Squire notched Rolf's ear to mark him as a thief. Rolf ran away and hasn't been seen since.

"My older brothers Alan and Botolph followed a Crusad-ing knight to the Holy Land. I was the only boy left. By then

I was about twelve. My mother was getting too old to gather. There were three sisters left. The farmers had their eye on us. I couldn't steal enough to feed us all. We had to go out on the road. Even if someone saw me stealing, I would be gone before they came looking.

"The next winter almost finished us. Sleeping outdoors was hell. My mother caught a chill and died. One by one my sisters walked away . . . forever. Finally there was no one but me. I wandered about, begging and stealing, for years. I was caught a few times. I was horsewhipped. I was dunked in a dunking chair until I nearly drowned.

"Finally I heard about Rembert. Working here there's always something to eat, a dry place to sleep, and family you can trust. I never have to fight, leastways not unless I want to. Once I have you hardened up I'll fight you, Earl. I'm not a honorable man. I can't wait to break your little nose. I'd turn your head to mustard if I could get away with it. I hate you and your kind."

Bobby surveyed the camp, realizing that all the robbers must have stories like this. Surviving had taken all their energy. Bruise had never had the luxury of growing up. He was a six-foot baby. Bobby had had everything handed to him on a platter. Up in his castle he, too, had never felt the urge to grow up. Until he met Fahd.

Rembert set his men to work preparing the big attack. He told them they'd be storming a fortress, but he didn't say which one so word wouldn't get back to the Count. Rembert promised them silk and satin, gold and jewels. Not the usual sheep and turnips and old blankets.

Rembert had the men build eight ladders. These would be lashed together in pairs to make four ladders tall enough to reach from the muddy bottom of the moat to the top of the wall. They laid each end of the ladders on a two-wheeled cart. Now the ladders looked like a long wagon. They loaded hay on it. The ladders were completely hidden.

They built four rafts by lashing tree trunks together side-by-side. Then they took the rafts apart and loaded the logs onto carts. They looked like harmless loads of lumber.

The men studied sword fighting. Each man got a shield made from a barrel top. They had only a few swords, so they forged more.

Rembert had 132 men. He knew they would not be as orderly or well-trained as the Count's 50. But they would be tougher and more desperate. Rembert was also counting on the element of surprise – getting his men into the fortress when the Count's soldiers were sleeping.

The attack would take place in the middle of the night. The men practiced in the dark: assembling the rafts and poling them around the lake, assembling and climbing the ladders. They never got it 100% right, but eventually Rembert decided they were ready.

Rembert gave the mothers their assignments. The most trusted, experienced men would be in Rembert's personal squad. They didn't know it, but they would be going to the chapel, opening Sir Balsam's coffin and collecting the Halberdier's treasure.

Chapter XVI. The Plan Set in Motion

Rembert's first task was to sneak his men and equipment into Gambrell Town. It was autumn. The days were getting short. People wore wooly hats and scarves. On the roads, they leaned into the wind and kept their faces down. All of this worked in Rembert's favor.

He chose a Wednesday, market day in Gambrell. The roads were clogged with farmers, bringing their crops and animals to the market. The robbers emerged from their hideout in small groups. They started before sunrise, so no one would see where they were coming from. After years of banditry a few of their faces were well-known. Those men went in disguise. Rembert's disguise was to go without a hat. Everyone in the county knew his feathered hat. No one except Florizel knew he was bald.

Before he left, Rembert helped Fahd tie Bobby up. Florizel begged Rembert to be careful. Rembert begged Fahd to take good care of her. Fahd promised no harm would come to her.

On the road to Gambrell the little knots of men from Rembert's camp mixed in with the other farmers and craftsmen. Their carts of hay and lumber, drawn by patient workhorses, joined a long file of carts carrying barrels, chickens, firewood, cloth, furniture and other goods for sale in the market.

Once in Gambrell Rembert's men rented stalls from the Sheriff. They set outrageous prices for their lumber and hay because they didn't want to sell any. Under the top layer of logs was a layer of shields and swords. Under the hay were coils of rope to splice together the ladders and rafts.

Some of the robbers circulated idly through the market, buying a tray of berries or a mug of ale, flirting with the market women and kicking the market dogs. Many of them stopped in the church for a long nap after lunch.

Back in Rembert's cave, Fahd serenaded Florizel with some of her favorite songs. He concluded this program with the Song of the Shepherdess:

> I must pass through thin and thick.
> I must prove my worth.
> Before I ask this pretty chick
> To flutter down to earth.
>
> Off he went upon his way
> To start a finer life,
> in hopes that he'd return someday
> fit for such a wife.

Florizel noticed he was becoming flushed. "What's wrong, Freddy?" she asked with genuine concern.

"I can't stay here and let the other men do all the fighting. I'm going!" He slung his guitar over his back.

"What about the little Earl? What if he gets loose?"

Fahd bit his lip. "I'll take him with me. It's the only way." And he started untying Bobby.

"Freddy! This is not how Rembert planned it!"

"I can't hide in a cave like a woman. This was partly my idea! I helped to plan it!" By now Bobby's hands and legs were free. He jumped up.

Fahd said calmly, "Florizel, I promised to keep you safe. I know you'll try to follow us." He locked his arms around her.

"Tie her up, Earl!" Bobby picked up the rope and secured her wrists and ankles. Florizel was too surprised to resist.

Fahd looked at her earnestly. "Rembert would never forgive me if you got hurt. We'll be back tomorrow, even if we have to crawl." He put his hand on his heart. He meant it.

He put some food and drink within reach, threw the Turkish carpet over her and led Bobby to the cave entrance. "Let's not say good-bye. We'll be back."

Florizel shrieked, "What are you up to, Freddy? There's something fishy going on! Eek!" Freddy gave her an apologetic look and led Bobby away.

Once they were out of sight the two broke into big smiles and hugged each other. "So far so good," said Fahd. "Now comes the hard part." At the far end of the lake Fahd dug out the goatskin containing their disguises. Some spiders had nested in the clothing, but it was dry.

Fahd put on the monk's robe. Bobby put on the dress and hooded cape. Then they climbed up to the high road. The hoods left their faces in shadow. They joined a group of women heading to the market to buy provisions. Fahd held Bobby by the wrist as if he were dragging him against his will.

"Good morning, Brother," said one of the women.

"Good morning," said Fahd in a low, serious voice.

"Do you need any help?" asked the woman, trying to get a glimpse of Bobby's face. The other women blushed with embarrassment.

Bobby chose this moment to tug on the monk's hand, slowing him down. Fahd yanked him forward. "It's a rum story, Missus. This is my sister Meg. She's an ill-tempered girl who's been tormenting our mother ever since she was old enough to break things."

Bobby dug in his heels again and Fahd yanked again. "She must spill things and she must taste things. She must kiss the lads and get her clothes dirty. There's nothing she hasn't tried. She has eaten worms. She has climbed trees with no knickers on."

"My, my," the ladies clucked, observing Bobby's rough, brown hands and scuffed shoes. Bobby tried to twist out of Fahd's grip.

"I'm putting her in service. In Gambrell. She can do scullery work in the Count's household. That is, if they'll have her."

"My Angela was difficult," piped another of the women. "She *would* run away and she *would* play with boys. Had to hunt rabbits. Had to dig moles. Dirty? Disrespectful? Oh, my. Didn't get over it till she fell in love. *Then* she wanted to be a girl. Now she and Devere have their own problem, Little Autrey. Always hitting." She shook her head.

And so the conversation went, all the way to town. It was getting close to noon when Fahd and Bobby and their gossipy companions reached the marketplace. Glancing around, Fahd could see that Rembert's plan was working. There were familiar faces scattered through the crowd. The wagons were pulled up along the moat, their loads intact.

Fahd and Bobby drifted through the market. When they came to the palace drawbridge, Fahd dragged Bobby across to the palace gate. He had no surefire plan for getting in, only a few ideas.

A little window in the gate swung open. "Who are *you?*" asked the soldier guarding the door.

"Brother Carl for the Bailiff," answered Fahd.

"About what?"

"It's this girl," said Fahd. "It's Meg."

Curious, the soldier sent word to the Bailiff. A few minutes later the message came back, "He don't know a Meg." Fahd and Bobby started to sweat.

"That's very true," said Fahd. "Very true. This ain't Meg. It's the Bailiff's daughter. Tell him that."

This maneuver *did* bring the Bailiff to the gate, hopping mad.

"What's this supposed to mean," he demanded with a red face. "This is no daughter of mine."

Bobby lifted his hood just enough so the Bailiff could recognize the naughty boy he had punished a few weeks earlier. The Bailiff's anger turned to disbelief. Fahd lifted his own hood and said, "I am the Tunisian singer, sir. We have something very important to tell the Count. The marketplace is full of robbers, planning to raid the castle. Please let us in. If they spot us talking to you we're dead meat."

The Bailiff, who was a decent man, could see that Fahd was actually afraid. He also remembered that Bobby, though horribly disrespectful, had been honest.

Seeing the Bailiff hesitate, Fahd went on. "Let us tell our story. Afterwards, if you see fit, cast us out again. But as long as we stand here we are in mortal danger."

The Bailiff nodded to the guard, who admitted them. They threw off their hoods and thanked the Bailiff with all their hearts.

Fahd took a deep breath. "In Medwickshire, just north of here, there is a bold robber band. Decent folk live in fear of Rembert the bandit. No one sleeps soundly. They are always half-listening for the sound of hoofbeats, the sound of Rembert and his men. Chickens are wrenched from their perches, daughters scream with fear, beds and cupboards are dragged out and carted away. No one, no matter how humble, is safe from Rembert. Perhaps you've heard of him?" Fahd was visibly sweating.

The Bailiff nodded gravely. "Rembert the Ruthless."

"We just escaped from Rembert. We were captured on the road and dragged to his camp. We escaped because Rembert and all his men came here this morning." Fahd paused to make sure the Bailiff was paying attention. "They are out in the market now. Their mission is to storm this fortress."

The Bailiff stiffened and turned to the guard. "Muster the men. Now!"

"Please hear me out," pleaded Fahd. "Don't attack them now. They'll just run away." The Bailiff looked into Fahd's eyes, trying to decide whether to believe him.

Fahd met his gaze. He went on, "I know what they're planning. They've been practicing for weeks. I have my own plan to prevent bloodshed, save the fortress, and free Medwick forever from these men's raids. We have time to talk this over, if you and your Lord are willing. The attack is scheduled for midnight."

The Bailiff scratched his head. "I'll speak to the Count," he said, and left them standing in the courtyard. Then he returned to say, "You'd better come with me."

The Count was in the drawing room playing checkers with his son. He looked up with mild annoyance when the Bailiff appeared at the door. When he recognized the Bailiff's two companions his annoyance increased. His son stood up indignantly.

"Father!" said Tristan. "This is the naughty boy! The one with all the cheek!"

The Bailiff approached the Count and whispered a few words into his ear. The Count's eyebrows went up. He examined Fahd and Bobby with greater interest. Finally, he beckoned them to approach.

"First, how do we know you aren't part of the robbers' scheme, sent here to mislead us?" His tone was not unkind. The Count of Gambrell was, in fact, wise and just.

"You can watch the bandits from the top of your walls," said Fahd. "Rembert has 132 men. Tonight after dark, they will assemble rafts and ladders. They will throw their ladders against the wall and climb into the fortress. I'm not asking you to surrender. I'm asking you to lure them into the courtyard and trap them. Then you can judge them and deliver justice. I have a strong personal reason for plotting Rembert's downfall. My whole future depends on it."

The Count and the Bailiff, each studying Fahd's face intently, had another whispered consultation. They noticed that Bobby was maintaining a respectful silence, his hands joined behind his back. If the naughty boy had nothing to add, this might be true.

"How would it work?" asked the Count.

"Daddy!" said Tristan in protest. But the Count ignored him.

Chapter XVII. The Assault

Rembert was not in the market. He was hiding in the home of Alf, a former member of his band. Alf had a new racket: he sold a purple syrup that was supposed to ease the pain of childbirth. Rembert's men reported in regularly from the market. The wind was blowing. This would help cover the sounds of his operation. The cloud cover was fairly constant. Rembert did not want the moon popping out.

It seemed to Rembert that the day would never end. When the shadows finally got long enough he went to the market to take charge. At the sight of him the men broke into smiles. He frowned to remind them they weren't supposed to know each other.

One by one the sellers of dried peas and herbs and knitted nightcaps packed their things and went home. When darkness fell there were only ten or twelve carts left, including Rembert's hay and lumber wagons. The robbers were keeping out of sight, napping under bridges, playing cards in taverns or hiding in henhouses. They weren't supposed to gather until an hour past sunset. All those strapping men standing in the marketplace might attract attention.

When darkness fell the townsmen shuttered and barred their windows. Two or three fires flickered up in the marketplace. Men stood around the fires, rubbing their hands for warmth. Rembert's men began to drift in. Soon each campfire had an outer ring of bandits. At a nod from Rembert, his men passed jugs of grog from hand to hand. Before long eleven tipsy farmers found themselves surrounded by 132 frowning ruffians. Rembert stepped into the firelight.

"Friends, I'm Rembert the Ruthless from up Medwick way. I am engaged in an undertaking tonight. You have the bad luck to be in my way. If you cooperate you'll be home with Mum and the kids tomorrow. Here is what I ask. Sit quietly around the fire and notice nothing. My men will be at work behind you. If a voice is raised, my men will silence it. If a man gets up, my men will fell him. By morning we'll be gone. Any questions?"

One of the farmers, a big shambling man, seemed insufficiently afraid. Rembert pulled the sword from his belt and sawed off the man's collar button. "The next time it will be your nose," he said matter-of-factly. He turned and walked into the shadows. The farmers looked at each other and gulped.

Rembert strode to the edge of the moat and sized up the situation. It was still early. Bustle in the marketplace would cause no alarm. The wind was blowing steadily, banging loose shutters, whistling around the houses, masking most sounds except the insistent barking of a dog. Just then the fortress drew up its drawbridge. It was time. Rembert gave three short whistles. His men sprang into action.

They pushed the hay off the long cart and unloaded the ladders, lashing them tightly together to reach the top of the wall. They unloaded the logs, laid them side by side next to the moat and lashed them together into rafts. When that was done, they pushed four rafts into the water. On each raft they laid a ladder and two poles. Then they went back to the fires to wait. Their handiwork, riding low in the water, was completely invisible. The farmers stretched out and went to sleep around the campfires.

Rembert and his men waited for the middle of the night. They recounted stories of successful robberies to stoke their courage. They mused sadly about their raw bachelor lives.

After an hour or two all signs of life in the town died away, even the barking dog. Rembert signaled his men. They got up, stretched to get their blood flowing, and lined up to collect their swords and shields. Then they split up into four groups and gathered at the moat. Each raft held ten or twelve men. No one in the band knew how to count past five. So at first too many men crowded onto the rafts, causing them to fold and buckle. Half the passengers were tossed into the moat.

The men endured this without a word of complaint, just as they had during practices at the lake. Once enough of them had fallen off and the rafts became stable, raftsmen poled them across the moat to the walls. Each raft raised its ladder against the wall. They saw with relief that the tops of the ladders reached above the wall. And that no one seemed to be standing guard.

In the effort to raise a ladder one raft tipped over. The men found they could stand up in the moat with their chins above the water. Eventually they got their ladder, the fourth one, up against the wall. That was the sign the men were waiting for. Forty men scrambled up the ladders to the top of the wall. Forty men looked back down at their mates and signaled there was no one there. The raftsmen went back for another load of men. Another load of men crossed, climbed the ladders and joined their friends atop the wall. The plan was working.

Rembert was the first one up. He scanned the Count's residence for signs of life. It was dark and quiet. There were no guards in the courtyard, no guards on the walls. The setup was almost too perfect. Although it was too dark to see clearly, Rembert could tell that Fahd's description of the castle had been wrong. He could see arrow slits in the castle walls, to defend against enemies in the courtyard. The castle door was made of heavy wood with iron bands. The lower windows were high above the ground and shuttered. Fahd was no soldier. He must not have noticed these things. In any case, thought Rembert, if the Count felt so safe that he posted no guards, there would be no trouble getting into his castle.

The last forty men ran up the ladders, followed by the raftsmen. All the raiders now crouched atop the wall, weapons and shields at the ready. Rembert rose and led his men to a corner tower. He knew he would find a staircase there. But the door to the tower was locked. Rembert tried the tower at the other end of the wall. Also locked. He whispered to his four crew leaders. Each crew cautiously raised its ladder and dropped it inside the wall. Rembert gave a low whistle and the men swarmed down into the courtyard. They looked warily around, swords poised.

Then Rembert's beautiful plan started to fall apart. Above them, the doors to all the corner towers banged open. Men in armor poured onto the top of the wall. The first thing they did was grab the ladders and pull them up out of the courtyard. One of Rembert's men grabbed one and tried to hold it down. The Count's men simply lifted him up. He had to let go and drop back down to the ground.

Rembert looked desperately for a way out. They were as neatly penned as a herd of goats. He ran to the fortress gates. They were padlocked. Though he sliced at the big rusty locks with his sword, they would not open.

The men atop the wall stared down, silent. Rembert ran to the front door of the castle – the Count's residence. That door, too, was locked up tight. He thrust his sword into the crack and tried to lever the door open. His sword, made from soft iron, bent like a pin. "Damn!"

A flame appeared above them. A man with a torch had walked out onto the wall. He was wearing a knight's armor. He waited for Rembert's men to stop milling around. When they were all looking up, he spoke.

"I am the Count of Gambrell. You are now my prisoners." Rembert's men cursed and groaned, Rembert loudest of all. "I am going to leave you there till the fight has gone out of you. Then we will talk. I think you will find me a generous and fair-minded man." He went back into the corner tower and the door closed behind him.

Rembert sank to the ground in despair. He tried and failed to think of a way out. One after another, his men sank down too. Before long they were all sitting on the ground, staring at their hands. After an hour or two they went to sleep, leaning against each other for warmth.

They were awakened by the twittering of birds. The sky was a pale blue. They rubbed their eyes and remembered where they were. Far above them the windows of the castle opened. Curious heads leaned out and studied them. First the serving girls, then the butler, eventually fine ladies in conical hats.

Rembert and his men couldn't think of a word to say. Not to each other. Not to the fine ladies. Finally Bruise spoke up: "I'm hungry." Many of the men grumbled in agreement. They waited for a few more hours. To relieve themselves, they formed a circle and took turns urinating inside it. For bandits, this was humiliating. The women they had hoped to drag away with them were watching them relieve themselves on the ground.

From the castle came the sounds of meals being prepared and eaten. Someone practiced the flute. Someone else hummed at her work. Here and there bells tinkled to summon a servant. Rembert was still trying to think of an escape plan. In the middle of the afternoon Bruise said, "I'm *very* hungry." Everyone agreed.

Fahd and Bobby had grabbed some sleep in the Count's kitchen. That morning they headed back to Rembert's camp to release Florizel. They left the fortress of Gambrell by a secret tunnel. When they reached the cave they found Florizel gnawing on her fetters. She looked up hopefully. "Well?"

Fahd untied her hands and ankles. He chose his words carefully. "Everyone is safe. But there was a hitch. They went in, but they didn't come out."

Florizel shrieked. "Rembert! He needs me!" A sudden suspicion stopped her cold. She gave Fahd a hard look. She looked at Bobby, who was not acting like a hostage. Then she lunged at Fahd's face, claws out. "Why ain't you with him? What's this lad doing here? You shopped Rembert!"

Fending her off, Fahd waited until she was calm enough to listen. "It will all turn out for the best, Florizel. You'll see. We're taking you to Gambrell."

"Oh no you ain't. No more tricks! Get out!" She ran to the campfire and extracted a blazing stick. Fahd and Bobby backed out of the cave. Once outside, they heard her break down sobbing.

Fahd hung his head. "I hate it when women cry."

"Me too," said Bobby, although he had never made a woman cry. They headed back to Gambrell to see how the Count was doing.

Chapter XVIII. A Future for Rembert

By midafternoon, when the robbers were *very* hungry, the Count went back out on the wall.

Rembert and his men rose slowly to their feet. They had given up on escaping, but they had not lost all hope. This was the mood the Count was waiting for.

"Good afternoon," he said cheerily. "I think we can talk now. I'll tell you what I propose. Please discuss it among yourselves and give me your answer later." The men in the courtyard strained to understand him. "I believe I am addressing Rembert – Rembert the famous bandit?"

The men gave a halfhearted cheer.

"I am not inclined to punish you for climbing into my fortress. After all, you haven't committed any crime." The men looked at each other in surprise. "Still, it's inconvenient having you all in the courtyard. It's starting to smell. I can't hold you here much longer. However," the Count went on, "I can't let you go. You would go back to robbing. The people of Medwickshire, your own neighbors, would never forgive me. If I'm wrong about that, please correct me." No one disagreed. He paused to let the truth of this sink in.

Rembert cleared his throat. He was going to promise to change his ways. It was a lie, but lying was a habit. The Count didn't give him time to speak.

"I see a way out. I didn't think of it myself. One of your men suggested it to me – the singer Freddy." This was greeted with shocked silence. "I thought poorly of him before." The Count was speaking honestly. "Now I see his worth."

"Some fifty years ago Christian knights fought their way into the holy city of Jerusalem, to free it from heathen rule. Now it is threatened again. Pope Eugene is organizing a new crusade. You are sinners, but you are fighters. By fighting in this new crusade you could earn forgiveness for your sins."

The Count was going too fast. The faces below him were blank. So he made it simpler.

"My cousin, the Duke of Northumberland, is looking for soldiers. I am asking you to join his army." The bandits perked up their ears. "He will be going to the Holy Land, the land of Jesus and the prophets, to drive out the heathens. Heathens are men who have never been baptized."

Shock: "Never been baptized!"

Warming up, the Count went on, "The heathens tore down the Temple of Solomon and built a mosque in its place. They do not observe the sacraments, do not touch alcohol and won't eat pork."

To a man the robbers thought, "Thank God I'm English!"

"In the land where Jesus walked, men are praying to Mahomet!"

"No!" shouted Bruise.

"Not if I can help it!" shouted Shorty and Rocky.

"I am with you," said the Count. "It *shall not be*. Not as long as one Englishmen is left on God's good earth!"

"Hurrah!" shouted the bandits.

"The campaign will be long. You will have to walk to Jerusalem, halfway round the world. Are you soft and comfortable men, reluctant to leave home, fearful of hardships?"

"No!"

"The Duke wants men who are hardened by years of outdoor life. Men who have nothing to lose. Men who will fight like tigers! Are you such men?"

"Aye!" Shouts, oaths, dancing around.

The Count dropped his voice so the men would have to listen closely. "There will be no help from home. Crusaders have to rustle up their food in the countryside and get the local people to take them in."

The bandits turned to each other joyfully. Sounds like robbing!

The men's eyes glowed. When they were boys, they had not planned on becoming criminals. Now they could become heroes.

The Count concluded with a brief prayer. The men fell to their knees. Many grizzled cheeks glistened with tears.

"I now ask you to take counsel among yourselves. When you have decided what to do, call for me." The Count turned and disappeared.

There was a long silence while the men took stock of themselves. Were they ruffians? Or were they brave? They looked around, trying to read each other's faces. Then Rembert spoke up. "We'll go!"

"Aye!" shouted the men.

"Call the Count!" cried Rembert. As he waited he dreamed of Florizel. At that very moment her voice floated over the wall.

"Rembert! Rembert! It's me! Flo!"

"Flo!" he shouted back. "We're going on the Crusades!" The men threw their hats in the air and cheered. It was probably just as well that Florizel couldn't make herself heard. Alone at the edge of the moat she said to herself wryly, "What did he buy this time, a bag of magic beans?"

The Count reappeared. He was pleased with the bandits' decision. He introduced his Bailiff, who would tell them what to do next. With a smile and a wave he withdrew.

Unlike the Count, the Bailiff wasn't wise and just. But he knew how to give orders. "Men," he began, "you will stack your weapons in the far corner of the courtyard, on the other side of the castle. You will then return to this spot. Understand?"

Rembert and his men were ready to don the white robes of angels. They complied.

"Men," said the Bailiff when they got back, "the serving maids will now circulate among you with food and drink. You are not to grab, kiss or paw them. Understand?" Rembert's men laughed and consented with a single voice.

And so began a new chapter in their lives. Before leaving for the Holy Land they spent a month in training with the Bailiff. Winter was on its way. But they had warm lodgings. They drilled in the town square every day. Rembert and Florizel could see each other, but never had a chance to speak.

At the end of the month the men received crusader tunics – loose white blouses with red crosses sewn across the heart. Escorted by the Count's men, they marched out of fortress one brisk winter morning to join the Duke of Northumberland's army. A crowd of townsmen cheered them on. Florizel was among them. She ran alongside the column, keeping pace with Rembert. "I'm coming! I'm going with you!"

Rembert smiled at the thought. Then he frowned. "You can't come, Flo. It will be too hard for a woman."

"Not for me, Rembert. You know me. A campfire's all I need. And you."

Rembert knew this was true. He was moved by her loyalty and her love. He stepped out of formation, swept her up and seated her on his shoulders. Then he rejoined the marchers with a big smile on his face. The Bailiff smiled too, happy for another sign that Rembert's heart was good.

Fahd and Bobby watched from the back of the crowd as the men strode out of sight. Fahd wished Rembert and Florizel well. The Great Deed had not harmed them. And it had liberated the farmers of Medwickshire.

Chapter XIX. Settling Up

As soon as Rembert and his men marched away Fahd and Bobby headed north to Medwick. They scanned the hillsides for Ennis and her flock, but failed to spot her from the road. So they split up. Bobby went to Ennis's village, Creegan's Hollow. Fahd kept going up the high road to Medwick.

There was no sign directing travelers to Creegan's Hollow. In any case, Bobby couldn't read. He asked other travelers for directions. They told him to look for a cart path "on yer left, a ways past Rippler's Stream but below Windy Summit. Ye'll see a ruined cottage off in the distance with a dead tree." He found it. The day was getting late. He hoped he would be welcome.

The path wound around the side of a big hill checkered with fields and pastures. He heard the clanking of a faraway animal bell. Before long sheep came into view, treading the freshly fallen snow into mud. To Bobby's great delight, the person clucking her tongue to keep them moving was Ennis.

Ennis smiled at the sight of him: "The boy who's interested in sheep! Where's your friend?"

She remembered him! Bobby's mission was delicate. He was honored that Fahd had entrusted him with it, but afraid he would mess up. "My friend, Fahd, has business in Medwick Town. He sent me to look for you. Will you put me up tonight?"

"Of course." Ennis smiled. "Why would your friend be looking for me?"

"If I told you," thought Bobby, "you'd cuff my ears." So he gave the answer he had rehearsed. "He wanted you to have some news of him, and to make himself known to your father."

"My father?" asked Ennis with mock solemnity. She wasn't making Bobby's job any easier.

"Since we met you on the road a lot has happened. Can I tell you about it after dinner? In case you've forgotten, my name is Bobby."

"All right, Bobby," she said. For the rest of the way to Creegan's Hollow they talked about the weather, the harvest and the King's health. Ennis was so openhearted, so cheerful and so lovely that Bobby's heart melted all over again. Ennis's mother, when they reached the cottage, was a lot like Ennis, though her hair was flecked with gray.

Bobby was seated by the fireplace, nursing a hot cup of broth, when Ennis's father pushed through the door. He looked as rugged as a tree. "Who's this?" he demanded. "News? From the boys?"

"No, Dad. He's someone I met, out with the sheep."

The father, whose name was William, sank into his own big chair. He eyed Bobby suspiciously. "What is it, then?" His hands, resting half open on the arms of his chair, were big enough to throttle a bull.

Bobby's mind went blank. Ennis helped him out. "He's a friend, Dad. He stopped by on his way to Medwick. To say hullo."

"Oh," said William, and went out to wash up. The evening meal was simple and good, groats and vegetables in a clarified beef broth. For dessert they had dried apples. Then they settled round the fire to hear what Bobby had to say.

"My friend Fahd is an unusual man," he began. He told them that Fahd was a farmer's son who had wandered the world in search of a place to settle down. That Fahd made his living as a singer and doctor. That people loved him for the beauty of his voice and the help he freely gave. Bobby noticed that William was going to sleep.

He jumped ahead. "When passing through this country a few weeks ago, Fahd was struck by two things. One was the people." Bobby gazed at Ennis, searching for the right words. "The people he met here were straight and strong and . . . beautiful. Fahd saw he could be happy here."

Ennis did not seem to get the message. "The other thing he noticed . . ." Bobby raised his voice to prod William awake, ". . . was that the district was plagued by a cruel robber." William opened his eyes. "Fahd decided to rid the country of Rembert the Ruthless." William laughed at this.

"Because he is a stranger, Fahd was worried he would not be welcome here. People would ask, 'Is he just a wandering vagabond? Or is he a man of substance, worthy to be one of us?' If he could rid the country of Rembert, he thought, people might accept him." Again William snorted.

"This is what he did." Bobby told the story. They paid close attention. Even Ennis was absorbed. When Bobby got to the end – Rembert's departure for the Holy Land – the family smiled at each other.

"I thought it was odd there had been no raids," said William. "Damned odd." He shook his head in happy disbelief. "You aren't just making this up?"

Bobby answered, "Fahd is in Medwick today inviting people to visit Rembert's camp – to get back their lost things. He will do his best to see that each man gets his own, and nothing more. If you go to the camp tomorrow you'll meet him, and see for yourself that the story is true."

So William did. He wasn't sure he dared to enter that notorious forest. But when he got to the turnoff, dozens of other honest farmers were heading the same way. In Rembert's camp it was easy to recognize Fahd. He was the man solving problems. Whose cartwheel was it? Whose seed grain? He delegated one of the farmers to ladle out a measure of stolen grain to all comers until the supply was gone.

William observed all this with satisfaction. He found an old shovel that had disappeared from his farm one night. He waited until Fahd was free and introduced himself.

"It's a great thing you've done for us. Thank you. I'm Ennis's father."

Fahd was so happy and relieved that he gave William a hug. William did not suspect that the Great Deed had been done entirely for his benefit. "When my work is finished here," said Fahd, "I would like to visit your village. Do you mind?"

"Not at all," said William. "Your friend Bobby is already there."

Chapter XX. Meetings and Partings

During the next two days Rembert's camp was thoroughly picked over. Fahd spent two nights in the cave, shivering under Florizel's carpet. On the third day someone claimed the carpet. Snow fell that day, covering the broken odds and ends that still littered the campsite. Three latecomers appeared in the clearing, glanced around, and went home. Fahd was the last one to leave. His pockets were empty. He had nothing to show for his time as a robber. But his heart was full of hope.

Once he turned off toward Creegan's Hollow, however, his nerve started to fail. Would Ennis still be the girl he remembered from the summer, as lovely as a picture? Had she found a boyfriend, or left the village? By the time he saw plumes of smoke rising from Creegan's Hollow's twelve cottages, Fahd's heart was pumping so hard his ears were red.

He tried the wrong door at first, and was sent to William's cottage. Ennis's mother was expecting him. "Ennis and Bobby should be home from the fields soon. Sheep don't go far in winter. Make yourself at home . . . Ferd, is it?"

"Fahd, Mum. Rhymes with cod."

"Fahd. I'm Rose of Sharon. Pleased to meet you. Bobby told us all about you. Very bold. William was happy as anything to see the robbers gone."

"I hope Bobby hasn't been a nuisance. He's never had a proper family, so he's a bit rough."

"Oh, we love Bobby. He's like a brother to Ennis." Rose of Sharon got a faraway look in her eyes. Fahd saw that she was thinking of her sons. He was glad Bobby had made a good impression. And a little jealous.

William arrived next. It was obvious he was pleased to see Fahd. He wouldn't let Fahd shake a dirty hand, so he ducked outside to wash. Then came the bleating of sheep and the shouts of two herders. Fahd rushed out to greet them. Bobby gave him a hug, but Ennis went to put the sheep in their pen. She greeted Fahd with a friendly smile, as she had before. If she guessed his feelings, she wasn't showing it.

"All the folks around here are very thankful," she said simply. "It's a great thing you've done."

"Me and Bobby."

"How could that be?" Ennis gave Bobby a mischievous smile. "Him being so young." Bobby punched her. Immediately regretting this, he patted the spot. Ennis laughed. Fahd blushed.

William appeared, red and wet, to usher them inside.

That evening everyone was jolly and relaxed except Fahd. Up until now he had glided through life making friends and spreading good cheer. Tonight he felt like a stuttering fool. Ennis was just as he remembered her. She was friendly and nice to everyone. This made Fahd suffer. Up on the mountain her sweet smile had made him feel they were meant for each other. Now he saw that it was her normal everyday expression. It made him love her even more. But it also made him feel selfish and clumsy for daring to claim her.

If Ennis was as nice as Fahd thought (and she was), she had some idea what he was suffering. But it wasn't her way to flirt, or whisper, or play games. The next morning she invited Fahd to help her and Bobby with the sheep. His heart lifted. It sank again when he saw how intimate she and Bobby had become.

To Fahd's delight, his and Ennis's strides matched. They found themselves walking side by side. Ennis was so natural, so calm, that he felt no need to make conversation. They just walked along together. She pointed out a rookery on a distant hilltop. He noticed that the lambs were half-grown. Before long he was smiling as freely as she was.

Bobby trudged behind them, or ran off to explore, or chased stray sheep. He was happy because he'd helped bring Fahd and Ennis together. The day went very fast. By the questions she asked, Ennis showed she'd thought a lot about Fahd's Great Deed. She did care about him and had a clear understanding of his worth. On the way home she slipped her arm through Fahd's, making him so happy his ears turned red again. He never had to give the speech he'd rehearsed. Fahd and Ennis were simply happy to be together.

Fahd asked if he could work on the farm. He didn't need to be paid. He was happy to work for food and lodging. William soon learned that Fahd was a good, resourceful worker. He slept in the stable and ate with the family. The whole family enjoyed his company. William spoke to the priest. A spring wedding was arranged. Fahd set to work learning about wheat and rye, fencing and drainage, sheep and chickens.

Bobby stayed on for awhile, pleased that everything had worked out so well. But there wasn't really room for him, and he wasn't really needed. He celebrated his twelfth birthday. Then it was time to go. The only sensible place to go was home. Once he told Fahd this, Fahd revealed to Ennis that Bobby was an earl. She thought it was funny. It made her like Bobby even more.

But the revelation shocked her parents. "An earl? Here? In this smoky hovel?" Ennis's mother burst into tears. She was a snob. She thought peasants, including William and herself, were low, unworthy creatures. That was why she'd sent her sons away from the farm.

"Your lordship!" she wailed to Bobby. "We are so ashamed! *So* ashamed."

Bobby told her how much he'd loved his time in Creegan's Hollow, how glad he was they'd liked him for himself, not for his noble blood. Rose of Sharon merely wept, twisting a corner of her skirt and dabbing at her eyes.

The day of Bobby's departure was a sad one. Everyone told him he'd be missed. He held them very tight.

And then he set out, alone and penniless, for home. Both he and his friends knew he could take care of himself. He had learned how to travel, how to get along with people, how to savor new discoveries. He wondered whether, further along the road, there might be another lovely shepherdess closer to his own age.

Chapter XXI. The Hermit

The high road was corrugated with hard frozen mud. Riders went slowly to protect their horses' hooves. Wind scoured the barren hills. Bobby whistled as he walked, but he would have enjoyed some company. When he caught up with a man in a billowing robe, he slowed down for a chat.

"Good day, sir," he said. The man, whose beard was blowing wildly in the wind, gave him a sideways look, then turned away. "Windy," Bobby observed.

The man looked at him again. "Of course it's windy. It's also cold. I don't care." He speeded up.

Bobby speeded up, too. "Why not?"

"How old are you?" replied the man. "Is there room in your head for anything besides pirate stories and fairy tales?"

"I'm twelve," said Bobby.

"Have you considered the Kingdom of God on Earth?" Bobby shook his head. The man stopped, gathered his robe underneath him, and sat down in the road. He glared straight ahead and waited for Bobby to leave. But Bobby stayed on, curious.

Reluctantly, the man got up. "The Kingdom of God on Earth is what Jesus promised to his followers – a world full of love and kindness. But people are still being cruel to each other. The only part of the world that is completely committed to Jesus is the Catholic church – the priests, the bishops and the pope. Is that what Jesus meant by the Kingdom of God on Earth?"

Bobby was not exactly following.

The man could sense Bobby's confusion, so he went on. "I am a hermit. I have been living by myself, talking to no one, for more than 13 years. In a hut. Praying and thinking. In all kinds of weather – scalding or freezing, wet or windy. A woman brought me a bowl of soup and a hard-boiled egg every day. I don't know who she was or why she did it. All that time I've been thinking about God's work. When will the whole world become his Kingdom?"

Bobby suspected the man was insane.

The hermit explained. "If God has the power to make the world better, what is he waiting for? Why does he let sickness and death, poverty and suffering go on for one more minute?"

Bobby did not know.

"When I finally saw the answer, I put on my shoes and went out into the world. I cleared my throat and spoke for the first time in more than 13 years."

"And what did you say?" asked Bobby.

"I'm saying it," said the hermit. "You're the first person I've met."

"What's the answer, then?"

"This" – the hermit spread his hands out, palms up – "is the Kingdom of God on Earth. We've been living in it all along." He looked intently at Bobby, waiting for his tremendous realization to sink in. Bobby looked blank, so he tried again. "*Everything* is the Kingdom of God on Earth."

Bobby saw he'd better say something, so he repeated, "On earth."

"*Yes*," said the hermit forcefully. "God made *everything*, bad and good. There's plague and war, but there's also freshly-churned butter . . . kittens . . . and swimming. We're not *waiting* for his Kingdom. Don't you see?" The Hermit made a sweeping gesture. "We're *in* it."

Bobby smiled. The hermit had spent 13 years working this out?

The hermit went on to quote Bible verses and cite church history, covering all the earlier theories about the Kingdom of God on Earth. The explanation took him two hours of steady walking, even though it was only a swift overview. He rubbed his chin. "For eight years the question got more and more complicated, more and more insoluble. Then a simple answer occurred to me, the answer I just gave you. I spent five more years working up the courage to believe it, because it is not what I learned in church."

"Uh-oh," thought Bobby.

The hermit stepped in front of him and grabbed his shoulders. "Are you shocked? Disgusted?"

"No," said Bobby. He resolved to ask an adult. In the meantime he smiled vaguely.

"Well," said the hermit, "that was easier than I thought it would be. Thank you, young man." .

"You're welcome," said Bobby.

Bobby and the hermit spent that night in a farmer's stable. They earned a meal and a place to stay by collecting eggs from the henhouse and mucking out the stable. In the morning Bobby set out again. The hermit stayed behind. He wasn't sure the farmer had fully grasped his great discovery.

The morning was gray and calm. An hour into Bobby's walk wet snowflakes began to fall. Around noon, he caught up with a woman and a half-grown girl, each with a basket. Their shoes were flimsy – soaked through and coming apart at the seams.

"Do you have far to go?" asked Bobby.

"Aye," said the woman. "Aye." And she gave the girl a concerned look.

"Mum," said the girl, "my feet are cold."

"I was thinking of taking shelter in a farmhouse," said Bobby. "Will you join me?"

"Can't," said the woman. "We're expected at Fuller's Crossing." The girl gave Bobby an imploring look.

"Just long enough to dry your shoes?" Bobby asked. "Till the snow lets up?"

"Oh . . . if there *is* someplace." But there wasn't a house to be seen. After half an hour or so they came to a little cluster of houses and sheds. One of the buildings, another stable by the smell of it, was standing open. Bobby peered in. It was dark and warm.

"Need any work done?" he called out into the darkness. "Currying, sweeping, feeding?"

A voice came from somewhere within. "This ain't an inn. It's a stable. The inn's next door."

"There's three of us," said Bobby. "We're cold and we have no money. Can we just dry off?"

"Not in here," said the voice.

Bobby stepped just inside the door and gestured to the others to join him. A man in a leather apron came out of the darkness, frowning. "Get out," he said.

"No," said Bobby. The man looked at the two women. He looked back at Bobby.

"Oh, suit yourselves." He jerked his head toward the fire crackling in a corner and returned to his chair. The other three stamped the snow off their feet, put down their loads and formed a ring around the fireplace. They took care not to block the ostler's heat. In the stalls a horse whinnied. A goat strolled up and nibbled Bobby's pants.

It was the ostler who broke the silence. "This your mum?"

"No," said Bobby. "We met on the road."

"This your sister, then?" asked the man.

"They're together," said Bobby.

"You all right, Missus?" asked the man.

The woman cleared her throat. "As right as anyone can be, whose husband has fool ideas and her son wants to throw away whatever little they have." The woman proceeded to tell her story.

Chapter XXII. The Man with Fool Ideas

"My husband is a baker up north. Our son, Garland, works as his baker's lad. Our shop, 'The Steaming Bun,' does a good business. We have a lovely home. Everything very nice. Cut flowers in summer. Stone floors throughout."

The daughter shook her head, remembering. The ostler was losing interest, scraping the dirt out from under his fingernails with a jackknife.

"The trouble started with our leftover, day-old bread. Farmers buy it for the pigs. There's good money in it. But my husband – Ken, he's called – he won't have none of that. He wants to give it to the beggars. 'They're going hungry, Mason,' he says. (My name is Mason.) 'Why give it to pigs?'

"'Because the pigs pay,' I said." She rubbed her thumb and forefinger together to emphasize this point.

"Ken comes back with, 'But how would you feel if you walked past The Steaming Bun without food nor money, starving?'

"'I'*m not* starving,' says I.

"'But what if you *didn't* have food nor money? Nor warm clothing nor a place to go?'

"'I *do*,' says I. My daughter here, Musk Rose, she's 13. She saw right away what Ken was getting at."

Musk Rose nodded emphatically. "I like nice clothes," said Musk Rose. "And tallow candles. And jam. That costs money. We can't go giving it away."

"Our boy Garland, now," said the woman, "he sides with his dad. 'Why give them *day-old* bread?' says he. 'Why not fresh?'

"'Where does it end?' I says. 'Why not invite them in? Here, take my wooly nightgown. I'll sleep on the woodpile.'

"'Would you let a man live worse than a pet cat?' says Garland. 'We've got plenty of room for a couple of beggars.'

"'Oh Lord, protect me from a Pharisee,' says I. 'They always knows best!' That's how it began." Musk Rose nodded vigorously.

"The next thing was Arfel. The bakery stays warm all night, see? From the oven? So Ken says to himself, he says, 'Why should this go to waste? A beggar could have the benefit of it.' And without discussing it with his wife, he invites a beggar to sleep in the shop.

"How do I find out? I go in there for some butter. It's dark. There's a smell of something. I step on something soft. 'Hey,' it says. 'Watch your step!'

"'Ken!' says I, 'we have an uninvited guest.' Ken comes in. Looks at the ground and sways back and forth. Not a word comes out of his mouth.

"'Get out of here,' I says to the bundle of rags. 'You smell bad.' And I wait for him to leave.

"Garland runs in. He stands between me and the dirtbag. 'No, Mum,' he says. 'Arfel stays.'

"'If Arfel stays, I leave.'" Musk Rose nodded emphatically.

"Ken says something like, 'Arfel is doing no harm.'

"'We *worked* for what we have,' says I. 'Arfel gathers dust. That's about what he does.' I did not walk out. Not then, anyways." Musk Rose nodded.

"The next night I peek into the shop. There is a pile of filth, snoring on the floor. I don't scream nor complain. I wait for Ken to explain things at dinner. We sit down to eat a fine fat fowl. Halfway through the meal the door from the shop slides open.

"'Mind if I join you? I'm feeling peckish.' It was Arfel, bold as a roof rat. Garland jumps up and offers him a seat.

"'I'd sooner die,' says I, 'than break bread with this ruffian.' I get up and leave the table."

"So do I," said Musk Rose.

"We watch from the doorway. Garland picks up the chicken carcass and hands it to Arfel. Arfel don't even bother to say 'Thanks.' Just starts gnawing. When he's done there's a circle of chewed-up bones on the floor. Does he slip away with a quiet 'Thank you?' No, he settles down and wipes his face on the table cloth.

"'I'm the kind of person,' says he, 'who enjoys hard work. If it's a chicken, I'll eat it down to the claws. If it's dancing, I'll dance till the band goes home. If it's chopping wood, I'll chop till it's too dark to see. My dad used to say, 'Arfel, why finish a chore? The faster you work, the more you'll have to do.' He was right, but that's not the Arfel way.'

"Even Ken has a hard time letting this pass. 'Well Arfel,' he says, 'it's interesting you mention wood chopping. I'll buy a tree from old Potter and you can pay us back by chopping it into firewood.'

"'Thanks!' says Arfel. 'I love a job like that. I love the sweat of it and the good ache afterward. If my back was strong, I'd start tomorrow morning. Fourteen years ago I was chewing a very tough piece of ham and my back popped out. I've had to go softly ever since.' He puts his hand in the small of his back and makes a face. 'Say, did I mention that my friend Shadrach will be staying in the shop tonight? For a brief while only. His daughter threw him out for drinking some ale she was saving for Easter. After Easter, Shad will go back home.'

"I scream, 'It's me or Arfel, Ken. Which do want as the companion of your old age?'

"Garland jumps up. 'Your old heart is colder than a door knob, Mother!'

"Ken jumps up. 'Now, Garland!'

"Arfel sits there as calm as you please. He says, 'Well now, Ken, if the missus leaves, do you suppose Shad and I could take the big bed as you won't be needing all that room?'

"That was all I needed to hear. Musk Rose and me are on our way to Mum and Dad's in Fuller's Crossing."

Chapter XXIII. News from Home

By the end of this story all three travelers had warmed up. They thanked the ostler and departed. Bobby wished Mason and Musk Rose the best of luck and hurried on ahead. At dusk he reached Beckham, only two days' walk from home. When he looked into the tavern he saw stacks and stacks of dirty cups. He paid for his bed by washing them.

It was there that he got his first hint about what was going on in Acton Waters. He was working at the pump in the courtyard, swabbing out cups by the light of a lantern. A stable boy stopped to chat.

"Where you from?" asked the boy, whose name was Ned.

"Acton Waters."

"Owww, Acton Waters," responded Ned. "Been away long?"

"I don't know. A few months."

"A few months! You don't know, then."

"Don't know what?"

Ned put his finger to his chin, hardly knowing where to start. "The earl there used to be a little snot in short pants. Was he still there when you left?" Bobby grinned. "Little wee fellow about eight years old? He was eaten by a bear. His sister is the countess now."

"Alison?" said Bobby with a start.

"Don't know her name," said Ned. "She is said to resemble a troll. She married a traveling salesman. *She* wants his love and affection. He wants her money. Now he spends every afternoon playing dice on the castle floor and every night with dancing girls."

"Dancing girls? In Acton Waters?"

"That's what I heard, yeah." Ned had never met a dancing girl. But he had a pretty good idea he would like her.

"Is that what they say?"

"That and worse," said Ned, getting wound up. "There's witchcraft . . . cattle rustling . . . people breaking out in a rash. The devil's playground, Acton Waters." Ned half-wondered what would come out of his own mouth next.

Bobby was shaken. He had barely thought about Acton Waters.

The next day he asked everyone he met about Acton Waters. He met a woman wrapped to the eyes in scarves. A puff of steam came out of the scarves: "Well, what I heard is, the Countess put on terrible airs. She would prance into town and step on people's necks. People don't mind Smooth (that's her husband). He don't do anything."

He met a sober gentleman in black. "Oh, Countess Alison. Her brother was a spoiled brat. People thought it couldn't get worse. Then the sister came and it *was* worse. I heard she would make the people in the village lick the sweat off her horse."

"Eeew," said Bobby involuntarily.

"She married a gambler," said the gentleman. "He flashed his teeth and claimed he was a marquess. Don't ask me what goes on in that castle now. She let all the servants go. It's not clear whether she even collects the rents."

"Uh-oh," thought Bobby.

He next caught up with a slouching man who wouldn't look him in the eye. This man said he was a footman seeking work. "The Earl – little Bobby – he kept three or four girls from the village locked up in a special chamber they called 'the

Cattery.' They was his pets, like. He never let soap touch his body. They kept that castle warm by burning his old clothes, which he wore until the lice ran out. He lost the throne in a game of cards to a beggarman. He run off and has not been seen since.

"The beggarman married his mum. The two of them killed her husband. He – the Earl's father – was a fat slug. He barely whimpered when they drowned him. Then the beggarman got itchy feet. Him and his new missus went off to join a tent show. They haven't been seen since."

"That leaves the sister, who is now the countess, and her husband Smooth. They have locked themselves in the castle, where they fight like pit bulls all day. Nothing comes in. Nothing goes out. People say there is mushrooms growing on the furniture. All they eat is mushrooms – soups, stews, loaves and salads."

Bobby's last informant was a woman in a bonnet. When he asked about Acton Waters she smiled and said she hailed from there. When he asked about the Countess she clenched her teeth and said nothing.

"What is it?" asked Bobby. "Afraid to spread gossip?"

The woman looked around fearfully. "Afraid of the Countess," she whispered.

Bobby spent the night in Brown's Landing. He sought out the ivy-covered house where he'd stayed before. His host was glad to see him.

"You look much better, if you'll pardon my saying so. You're brown and fit. And you've grown." The two little boys were glad to see him, too, hoping for a new story. After dinner, when they were all in bed, Bobby began one:

"Once there was a boy with everything you could ever want: roast beef and gravy, jewels, servants, dogs, horses, soft feather beds. But the boy wasn't happy. There was something he didn't have."

"Mittens?" asked Pip, who had gotten some for Christmas.

"A sled?" asked Prothero, who was wishing for one.

"No," said Bobby. "He had those things. He didn't *know* what was missing. So he went out into the world to look."

"Did he find it?" asked Pip.

"Yes."

"What was it?" asked Prothero.

"It wasn't anything you can hold in your hand."

"Too big?" asked Pip.

"It wasn't a thing at all. It was a way of thinking. Instead of looking at people and wondering, 'What are you going to do for me?' It was looking at people and saying, 'Hi!'"

"Waah!" cried Pip.

"That's not a story!" said Prothero.

"I haven't gotten to the interesting part," said Bobby, and told them about Rembert the Ruthless. But the boys were already asleep.

Chapter XXIV. Father Anselm

Bobby was only a day's walk from Acton Waters. But it was not the place he had left behind. His sister was in charge. And his sister, he knew, had a grudge against him.

He needed a hideout so he could size things up before showing his face. If he wanted to be the earl again, he would need allies and supporters. But aside from his parents, he couldn't think of anyone in Acton Waters who liked him.

Then he remembered Father Anselm. Father Anselm was a good, plainspoken man. He lived alone in a cottage next to the church. A perfect hiding place! Hoping for the best, Bobby set out for Acton Waters.

The day was icy, clear and windy. All the travelers had their heads bent, hurrying toward shelter. Bobby kept his face covered. Once he thought about it, he didn't suppose anyone would want him back.

By mid-afternoon it was dark. Winter days are short in England. Bobby arrived in Acton Waters just in time for evening mass. Inside the little church the only light came from a few flickering candles. He settled down to wait. After twenty minutes or so an old women came in and sat down. Two more came in, lit candles and knelt before the altar. The candle wax smelled good. Bobby's pants and shoes were wet. The church was damp and cold.

Father Anselm emerged from a door behind the altar. He said mass, attended by a tousle-headed altar boy. He gave the benediction and went back through his door. The old women shuffled home. Bobby caught up with the priest at the door of his cottage.

"Father Anselm?" said Bobby.

Anselm was surprised to hear a stranger speak his name. "Yes?"

"I am a penniless traveler. Would you shelter me?"

"You can stay in the church. It's always open."

"I have a story for you," said Bobby.

"Who are you?" asked Anselm.

"Bobby. The Earl."

Anselm opened the door to his cottage and shoved Bobby in. There was a fire inside. There was also a housekeeper, busy making dinner. Bobby raised a finger to his lips, hoping to keep his identity secret. Anselm understood.

"Why not rest till supper is ready?" he said, leading Bobby into the bedroom. Bobby stayed there until the housekeeper had gone home.

During dinner Bobby told his story. Father Anselm studied him. He had never known a child as naughty as Bobby. This boy seemed to be a different person. Was the change real?

"Who's on your side?" asked Father Anselm. "Who wants you back?"

"Nobody," said Bobby. "I've heard that my sister married a gambler. I don't even know what's become of my parents."

So Anselm told him. Bobby's father had joined an order of fisherman friars. His mother lived a meager life in the castle with Alison. Soon after her marriage Alison realized George was a fake. All he wanted was her money. So she had become a miser, refusing to spend a penny. The two were no longer speaking.

George had moved into the gatehouse. He ran a casino there, offering mead, snacks and entertainment. Gambling debts had ruined several of the local farmers. The gatekeeper, along with all the other servants and employees, had been fired.

No one was collecting taxes. Half the people in town – the ones who used to work at the castle – were unemployed. There was no one to enforce the law, no one to settle arguments. No one fixed the roads; a dog could drown in some of the puddles. The castle was falling down. The horses were starving. Alison didn't care.

Bobby hoped he could fix things. Anselm shook his head sadly. "How do I know you'll be better than Alison? You used to be almost as bad."

"I don't know," said Bobby. "I'm only twelve. But I've grown up. I like people now, and people like me."

Father Anselm wondered whether Bobby was just telling him what a priest would want to hear.

Bobby guessed what Father Anselm was thinking. So he told about his first visit to the Count of Gambrell, when he was beaten for insisting that a beggar is as good as a count.

The two of them sat quietly, reflecting on this. Father Anselm didn't mind long silences. Most of his conversations were with God, who never says a thing.

It would be risky to take Bobby's side. Alison might fire him. His Bishop would tag him as a troublemaker. He would have to rejoin his family in the North, where they knitted caps and dishtowels for a living. "Oh, well," he thought. "At least I'd have my books." But his books – the Bible, a prayer book, and a pamphlet about the meaning of dreams – belonged to the Church. In those days books had to be copied out by hand. They were rare and valuable.

Suddenly he smiled. "I'll help," he said.

"Thank you!" said Bobby, and the two began to work on a plan.

Chapter XXV. Bobby!

Their first step was to get in touch with Bobby's mother. It was safe to guess she'd welcome her son back. She had been terribly worried when Bobby disappeared. Anselm paid her a visit.

"Lady Nelda," Anselm said "I have a plan for getting things back the way they were in Bobby's time. But I don't think the castle is a good place to discuss it." If Alison overheard them she would have a fit.

"Shall I pay you a visit, Father Anselm? Say, tomorrow afternoon?"

"Why not come for lunch? I can only offer bread and pickles, but my housekeeper makes excellent spiced wine."

Lady Nelda agreed. She was tired of spinach. Bread and pickles sounded pretty good. At noon the next day Father Anselm greeted her with a mysterious smile and stood aside to reveal Bobby.

"Bobby!" cried Lady Nelda, bursting into tears. Bobby stepped forward and hugged her. Into his hair she murmured "I thought you were dead!"

"Didn't you get my note?"

"What note? You can't write!" She stepped back and looked at him. "You're so grown up!"

"I'm glad to see you, Mom," said Bobby.

After more smiles, tears and hugs, the three of them sat down to lunch. Lady Nelda didn't think Bobby would touch brown bread and pickles. Oddly, he seemed to like them. Odder still, Father Anselm seemed to like Bobby.

Bobby told his mother about the note he'd sent from Beckham.

"It never got here," she groaned. "If it had, we never would have made Alison the Countess, and your father might still be here. A thousand sad things have happened since you left."

"Well here I am," said Bobby. "Ready to put things back the way they were."

Lady Nelda rolled her eyes. "Where have you been?"

Bobby told about Fahd, the man who turned left, Pip and Prothero, Ennis, the Great Deed, the Kingdom of God on Earth, Arfel, and much much more. Some parts of the story shocked Lady Nelda. She did not think beggars were as good as counts. Nevertheless, Bobby impressed her. He had become brave and generous! Maybe he *could* save Acton Waters!

Then it was her turn to tell about the search for Bobby, choosing his replacement, the vegetarian menu, Alison's high-handed behavior, George, and the departure of Bobby's father. "Alison stopped spending money. She stopped collecting taxes. She fired everyone but the cook. We eat weed greens from the courtyard. The only fire is in the kitchen; that's where we spend the day. The roof leaks. No one sees to things." Lady Nelda shivered.

"Where is Father, exactly?" asked Bobby.

"In a friary called 'The Fighting Trout.' They are fishing guides. Your father is now called Brother Alvin. Alvin is his name, it turns out. He told me it was 'Arturo.'"

Bobby had heard most of this before. He hadn't wanted to believe it. "Wouldn't Alison be glad to have me back? I could fix things."

"Would you stick to a vegetarian diet? Would you outlaw hunting? Would you take regular baths?"

"Probably not."

"Well." Lady Nelda shrugged. "You were mean to Alison. Things always had to go your way." Lady Nelda told about Alison's first day in power, when she out-Bobbied Bobby. "She turns out to be strong-willed."

"Oh," said Bobby. All three fell silent.

Bobby finally spoke. "I have to get the people behind me. Then I could overthrow Alison – in a nice way, of course."

"How?" asked Lady Nelda. "If Alison and George find out you're here, they'll drive you out of town."

"Hmm," said Bobby.

Lady Nelda had one idea. "If you could read and write, Bobby, we could exchange notes. No one else in Acton Waters can read. George can't even multiply by two. He once ordered five socks."

Father Anselm promised to spend the long winter evenings putting Bobby through first grade. Although she didn't quite believe it, Lady Nelda was pleased.

Father Anselm's housekeeper, Marilee, saw that Bobby was a decent, sensible lad. So Anselm dared to tell her who he was. She may have hinted some of this to her husband. Father Anselm heard rumors that Bobby was back.

Chapter XXVI. The Royal Legate

Bobby needed allies. So Father Anselm went to see Frog the Blacksmith, a man that everyone admired. Frog was not a learned man. He was not even particularly good-natured. But he feared no one and said what he meant. Anselm invited Frog for a walk so they could speak in private.

They began by agreeing that things had gone downhill in Acton Waters. Then Anselm dropped a bombshell. Word of their problems had reached London. The king had sent a spy – a royal legate – to investigate. If the legate recommended it, the king might replace Alison with a better ruler.

The investigation had to be conducted behind Alison's back. Common folk would be afraid to speak if there was any chance Alison might find out.

The Legate had thought of a way to learn the truth. People would come, one at a time, to the priest's cottage after dark. Anselm would be in church, saying mass. The Legate would stay in the darkened bedroom and speak through the door. No one would see the visitors or ask their names. If this worked as planned, the Legate would hear the truth, and no one would get in trouble for snitching.

"I want you to test this plan, Frog," said Father Anselm. "So I'm asking you to come to my house tomorrow before dawn, when I ring the bell for morning prayers. Speak to the Legate. See whether you can trust him. If you do, help me find others who will speak out."

Frog nodded. Father Anselm withdrew.

The next morning Frog knocked gently at Father Anselm's door. A voice invited him to come in and sit by the fire. Frog thought the voice was too high to be a man's. He suddenly realized the Legate was a woman trying to sound like a man. He vowed to watch his language. So did all the witnesses who followed.

"I don't know who you are and never will," said the voice. "I ask you to tell me the truth. Don't sweeten it or leave things out. Will you?"

Frog cleared his throat and agreed.

"What's going on?" asked the voice.

Frog was taken aback. He had expected the Legate to be roundabout. "Well, milady . . ." he began. Bobby did not correct him, though his feelings were hurt. Frog repeated what Bobby had already heard, with a few additions. George had debts in the town. He wasn't paying his bills. But farmers and tradesmen were afraid to ask him for money. "Sir George is the law around here," said Frog sadly.

"And who," asked the voice, "could get Acton Waters back in shape? What if the old Earl, Bobby, could be found?"

Frog held nothing back. "No, milady. That little popinjay was worse than Alison."

Before dismissing Frog, Bobby told him what the King had in mind for Acton Waters. To give the common folk more freedom. To reduce the taxes. A lord does best when his people do best, when the people are hopeful and work hard.

Frog found himself thinking that someone like the Legate, someone who listens to people, would make a pretty good replacement for Alison.

The Legate asked Frog to send the next witness that evening. Frog agreed.

The man he sent was Rolf. Frog chose someone who, like himself, was respected in the community, someone who always spoke his mind.

Rolf told how the farmers had suffered under Alison. Bad roads made it harder to harvest the crops. At the weekly market, merchants had to fight for a good stall. Merchants who cheated their customers were not punished. Some farmers were plowing and planting the common grazing lands, leaving less grass for the animals.

Rolf was especially bitter about Sir George. Two of his neighbors had gambled away their horses, their seed grain, even their beds. "George hasn't a drop of kindness in his heart."

"If Earl Bobby could be tracked down, could he remedy this?" asked the Legate.

"No, milady." Rolf had already discussed this question with Frog. "All he cared about was fun."

The Legate explained how Acton Waters might become a happy place. He asked Rolf to send another witness the next evening.

"Begging your pardon, mum. Was you looking for suggestions?"

"Yes," said the Legate patiently.

"Well, myself and some of the men has an idea."

"Yes?"

"Brown's Landing has a granary."

"Yes?" said the Legate.

"They save grain from good harvests to feed people in a bad year. The Earl sets aside some of the grain paid in for taxes. In a year with bad weather, it will keep people from starving."

"Oh!" said the Legate. "That's an excellent idea. Thank you." And he meant it.

The next witness, sent by Rolf, was a man who had been ruined by George. That was what he wanted to tell.

"I'm poor. I have nothing to lose. That's why I gamble. If I win I can save four lives – Margaret, me, and the babies. But every night I start by winning and end up cleaned out. Is that possible in an honest game?"

George didn't even bother collecting what the man had lost – a cold little cottage and some bare, greasy furniture. Instead he made the man and his wife work as butler and barmaid in his gatehouse. George didn't pay them. The only way they could eat was to steal food from George.

"He'll catch us. Oh, he'll catch us before long. Then what'll he do? Kill us? Why would he do that? *To show the others they'd better pay up.* That's why. To show the others."

The man was shuddering. No one could have been un-happier.

"This cannot go on," said the Legate. "If I do not save you, sir, may the Devil strike me dead."

Chapter XXVII. Sir George Receives a Visitor

Sir George's nights were busy with gambling, but his days were boring. No one came to gamble until dark; they were all doing farm work. So George was trying to learn the guitar. He had won one from a traveler. When that got boring he tried teaching his parrot to swear. He had won the parrot from another traveler. Much of the time he simply sat and looked out the window, wishing something would happen.

He perked up when a boy with a backpack appeared at his door.

"Yes?" he said with his usual smooth smile.

"Is this an inn?" asked the boy.

"Well, that would depend on what you mean," said Sir George. "This is a house of pleasant diversions, including games, food and drink. I am Sir George, your host." He bowed. "If you like hazard and excitement, please come in."

"I do," said the boy. He walked in and took a look around. George had made the gatehouse fairly comfortable. There was a big fire crackling in the fireplace. But in the corners of the room giant dust balls swayed lightly to and fro.

"When does the fun begin?" asked the boy.

"Well, if you have a little money and need more, we could roll the dice now. The other guests usually arrive after dark."

Bobby (for it was Bobby, although George had no way of knowing this) had no money. "I'll wait for the others," he said. "Do you mind if I warm myself by the fire?"

"Not at all," said George. He liked company.

"You're the lord of this town?" asked Bobby. "It's very nice of you to take in a humble stranger."

"Oh, no," said George. "This is not a castle, and I'm not the lord. My castle is in Long Billings, a few days to the south. The lord of *this* town is a girl named Alison, age 15. She hates this house of fun, and would kick me out if she could."

"Why can't she?"

"We're married," said George with a smooth smile.

"Oh," said Bobby. "But . . . ?"

"She's a baby. She has only one idea – don't eat anything with a tail on it." George laughed softly. He was pleased with himself.

"Funny that a young girl would be lord of this place."

"Inherited from her brother," explained George. "He drowned in a swamp at the age of 11. He was chasing a turtle."

"It's lucky you came along," said Bobby.

"Well, it is and it isn't," said George with a wink. "The people here have a fatal weakness for gambling. The day will come when I'll shake this town and nothing will jingle. Then I'll hop it."

"But how can you leave? Your wife is here!"

"My boy, a fellow like me can do whatever he wants! One day my child bride will look for me in vain! We're about as married as the fork and the spoon." George danced a little half-circle around the fireplace.

Bobby began to see that George was not a serious threat.

George sighed. "Nothing lasts," he said. "Sooner or later everything crumbles. Turrets, towers, walls. So it will be with me. In the end there will be no more Sir George. There will only be Sir Fungus." The thought moved George to quiet tears.

Bobby did not wait for Sir George's other customers. While George studied himself in the mirror, Bobby slipped back to Father Anselm's house.

⁂

During the next few days Bobby received more and more secret visitors. One was a woman who was having a hard time selling her angel food cakes. Fewer and fewer people were coming to the market, discouraged by the cheating and roughness. Another was a man who lived by renting out his team of workhorses. The farmers couldn't afford them any more.

People were worried about the commons, the grazing land shared by all. One visitor proposed that the castle grounds be included in the commons. Another said that the way to stop farmers from grabbing the common ground would be to help each one consolidate his scattered fields into a single farm.

Over the generations, farmers had divided their property among their children. These parcels had been further divided by grandchildren and great-grandchildren. The average farmer now had many scattered plots, some miles apart. A wise ruler could organize a land swap. People would swap plots until each farmer had one large field, like his ancestors.

There were silly visitors. One woman was angry because Alison had suspended the annual town Christmas party. Another wanted to plant roses around the town square. Another wanted his wife's specialty, a pudding known as "brown pudding," to be renamed "Ann's Pudding." A man wanted to reclaim a box containing his dead mother's hair, now in his sister's possession.

A young woman (Bobby knew it was Bronwen, the girl he had once loved) said Alison was an improvement over Bobby. Bobby had pestered her and threatened her boyfriend, Pete. When Bobby disappeared they finally dared to marry. "I don't think he's dead, your Honor," she said. "People have seen a boy around here that, if he's not Bobby, he's Bobby's twin. Please, milady, don't let him come back."

"Well, if he does come back," said the Legate, "I guarantee he won't bother you."

"Oh, Lord," groaned Bronwen. Bobby had heard enough. It was time to act.

Chapter XXVIII. Madam, with all my heart!

That evening Bobby asked Father Anselm to bring Frog back to the cottage. If Bobby was going to recruit a band of followers he would have to convince Frog, who knew everybody. It was going to be an important conversation.

Bobby seated himself in the bedroom. There was a knock on the door. From the darkness, Bobby invited the man in.

"Sir," Bobby said, "my investigation is complete. I am ready to do what I can." Frog listened quietly. "If my plan is going to work, I need the people behind me. I am going to outline my ideas. Will you tell me what you think?"

Frog cleared his throat and answered, "Yes, milady." He felt honored.

"First of all," said Bobby, "an earl's job is not just having fun. He must protect and support his people. Everything the earl has comes from the people. The earl will be well off when the people are well off. Do you agree?"

"Aye," said Frog.

"He can help people by punishing criminals, settling disputes, managing the market, maintaining roads and ponds, organizing a volunteer fire department and providing for other emergencies. One of those dangers is crop failure. To carry people through a bad year, the earl should collect and store grain in a public granary. Do you agree?"

"By God, yes," said Frog. His heart was beginning to swell with pride. "We, the ordinary folk of Acton Waters," he thought to himself, "have brought this lady around to our side."

"The people I talked to had other good ideas," said Bobby. "One of them is to help farmers exchange their tiny, scattered fields. If farmers can consolidate their holdings, they won't have to spend so much time going to and fro. Another good idea is to allow grazing on the castle grounds. Do these ideas sound good?"

"By all that's holy," said Frog in his deepest, gruffest voice.

"Sir George's gambling den must be closed. His winnings must be given back. The staff and soldiers at the castle must get their jobs back. The castle must be repaired. The annual Christmas festival must be revived, along with the Maypole Dance and Midsummer Night's Bonfire. Have I left out anything important?"

"No, milady," said Frog, who would have jumped up and done a jig if he had dared.

"Now we come to a delicate question," said Bobby. "Who should replace Countess Alison? I wonder whether I dare to propose myself." He went on quickly, "I am related to her."

Understanding the delicacy of this question, Frog jumped in. "Madam, with all my heart! If only Acton Waters could have a ruler like you!"

"Sir," said Bobby warmly, "May I count on your support?"

Frog slammed his fist onto Father Anselm's table. "My heart, my hand and my voice!"

"If we are to take the next step, I must leave the shadows. I must show myself to you. I will see you as well. Do you object?"

"Not at all, your ladyship!" Bobby stepped boldly into the light. Frog was struck dumb. He had formed a picture of a noble lady in a dove-gray riding habit, her hair tied up with pins. What he now saw was a 12-year-old boy. Then he received another shock. "Are . . . are you Earl Bobby?"

Bobby nodded gravely. "I'll explain why I'm back, and why I haven't shown my face. But first I want you to thank you for everything you've said. I am not the Bobby you knew before. Before, when I met someone, I thought 'What can you do for me?' Now I think, 'Hi!'"

Frog's mouth was hanging open. Realizing this, he closed it. He was experiencing a rush of emotions. Bobby had tricked him. Bobby saw the resentment in Frog's face. But he also saw hope. Frog's expression softened.

"So, my lord (if you *are* the earl) . . . if you wanted to take over again, the King would not have to choose you?" Bobby shook his head. Frog thought this over. "Why don't you just walk into the castle? What was all this play acting?"

Bobby explained that Alison would not give up. He needed the people's support. Before showing his face he would have to improve his reputation.

"By God, son (if I may call you that!), I want to believe you! I'm Frog, the blacksmith. Shall we throw in together?" He offered Bobby his scarred, massive hand.

"Frog," said Bobby, "I owe you more than I can hope to repay."

Frog immediately protested. "I want no special favors. That would not look right. The villagers would not like it and neither would I."

"It wasn't a reward I was thinking of," said Bobby with a smile. "I was thinking there's more I will ask of you, time and time again."

Just then Father Anselm returned from mass. He saw at a glance how things were going, smiled, and clapped Frog on his mighty shoulder.

"You see, Frog? You see why I joined the lad's scheme?" Frog gave a brisk nod and returned Anselm's smile.

Bobby explained his plan. If he could get the people of Acton Waters to march with him to the castle, Alison would see there was no hope for her. George, he already knew, would head for the hills. But how could he get the people behind him?

Frog had a ready answer. The farmers and villagers were buzzing about the Legate. "What we agreed – the ones I talked to – was, we support the Legate. We wanted to find out who you was and ask the King to put you in as countess."

Frog paused, embarrassed by this confusion about Bobby's sex. Bobby just smiled. "So," Frog went on, "if the people find out you was the Legate, you'll have your army. No question."

"We'll have to move fast," said Bobby. "Once people start talking, word will get up to the castle. Can we meet again this evening? I would like to move tomorrow."

Frog thought about this, and agreed. After handshakes all around, he walked purposefully off into the night.

Bobby sat down to write his mother a note. This is what he said: "Peepl march tumaro. Alz wel. Boby."

Father Anselm carried the note to Lady Nelda. She sat down and wrote, "Dear Bobby, I'm so glad things are going well. Alison still has no idea you're here. Here's hoping that tomorrow is the beginning of a new day for Acton Waters!"

Looking over her shoulder, Father Anselm kindly suggested that the note would be hard for his pupil to read. Lady Nelda threw it away and started over. Here is the note she actually sent:

"Boby, how wunderful! Yoor, mum."

Chapter XXIX. Long live Bobby!

The day of the revolution dawned cold and gray. The plan was to summon everyone to the village square. Bobby and Father Anselm went there at sunrise. Soon Frog appeared with five of his neighbors. There were hugs all around. The seven waited silently, facing outward to see whether anyone else would come. Over the castle, golden rays of sun shot out from behind the towering clouds.

They spotted a farmer and his wife coming along the high road, he with a hoe, she with a sickle. When the pair got close enough Frog recognized them as friends. He gave a great shout. The sound seemed to arouse many villagers who had been hesitating. They began to trickle in from all corners of the square. Farmers in knots of three or four appeared on the high road. All the newcomers were greeted with happy shouts, getting louder and louder as the crowd grew. People stood together and chatted, pleased to be taking part in a historic event.

Before long 200 people were milling around the square. Bobby went over to Frog, who lifted him up on his shoulders. Gradually the voices died down.

"I'm Bobby, as you probably know. I will never forget your help today, and I hope you will never forget what I owe you. Let's go to the castle!" The people cheered and formed a long column.

With Frog, Bobby and Father Anselm at the head, they marched along the high road toward the castle. Villagers saw them passing, put on their hats and rushed to join the procession.

By the time he reached the gatehouse, Bobby couldn't see the end of the column behind him. Inside the gatehouse, George pulled aside a curtain and peeked out. He spotted the boy who had visited him one afternoon. Who was he, and what was he doing at the head of a peasant army? Sir George shivered and locked his doors.

Someone struck up a song, a song that matched people's mood:

> I smell a southern breeze
> Soft and warm and clean.
> A hillside dark and damp
> Sprouting shoots of green.
>
> Hi ho the splashing waters
> Hi ho the flowers gay
> Hi ho a frozen country
> Born again today!
>
> Spots of golden sun
> Dance beneath the trees
> Swallows dart among
> The butterflies and bees.
>
> Hi ho the splashing waters
> Hi ho the flowers gay
> Hi ho a frozen country
> Born again today!

The men wore blue smocks, the women long brown skirts. Their cheeks were pink, their breaths made puffs of steam. They brought color into the drab castle grounds.

Alison heard them singing before she saw them. She was sitting by the kitchen fire, biting her nails. She ran out onto the stone platform that served as a porch. There she stood defiantly, legs apart, hands on her hips, one small girl against the people of Acton Waters.

"How dare you form a gang like this! I am your countess! Go away!" Lady Nelda appeared in the door behind her, smiling to see her son's supporters.

Bobby walked halfway up the steps. Seeing him, Alison shrieked. He gave her a smile and turned to face the crowd.

Alison pounded his back with her fists. "Get out of here, you little turd! You always get your way!"

Bobby didn't want to wrestle his sister. He was saved by Frog, who gently pulled them apart.

"Now, now, milady," Frog murmured.

"Men! Boys!" she cried. "Lady in distress!" She struggled. Frog had to lift her up, kicking.

"Bobby got better, Lady Alison!" shouted someone. "You got worse." Everyone cheered.

Mother Grace, who had once been Alison's nurse, climbed the stairs, took her from Frog, and hugged her.

Bobby raised his hand for silence.

"We can all work together, including Alison. As for George, well . . . let's go see." He led the people back down the drive. Alison wandered off sadly into the woods.

Bobby knocked on the gatehouse door. George opened a small peephole.

"Yes?" he asked smoothly.

"I'm Bobby, Alison's brother. The people have restored me as earl. Are you with us?"

"No," said George softly. "The people are about as intelligent as the wart on my ass."

Bobby spoke up so everyone could hear. "George, can we work together?"

There was a long silence. Then the door creaked open and George stepped out. He waved gaily to the crowd. There were some angry murmurs.

"Brother!" said Bobby, and hugged him. With a sickly smile, George hugged back.

Bobby turned to the crowd. "George and Alison can make a new beginning. They will live together as man and wife. Soon there will be nephews and nieces running around." George gave another sickly smile. He was looking around for a way out.

"I invite George rejoin his family. As for the rest of you, take a look in George's den. If you find something of your own, take it home!" Bobby threw the door open. George stood helplessly by.

Soon people came back out with things George had won from them – a quilt, a hairbrush, a stool, a hat.

Bobby linked arms with George. "Come to the castle, Brother!"

George's face resumed its smooth expression. "Not me," he said. "I'm leaving town."

"But my dear George," said Bobby mildly, "you can't just walk away. You have a wife here."

"I've been married to a woman in Shrewsbury for at least seven years. And I have two children in Drayton Combs. They need me."

Bobby called out to Father Anselm. "Father Anselm, what does this mean for Alison?

"Her marriage has no legal meaning. In the eyes of the church she is still single," answered Father Anselm. "How sad."

George ran into the gatehouse, emerging a few seconds later in his black velvet cloak. "I've got my dice," he shouted defiantly. "That's all I'll ever need!" And he fluttered off toward the high road.

"Three cheers for Bobby! Hooray! Hooray! Hooray!" cried the people of Acton Waters.

"Three cheers for us all!" cried Bobby. The people threw their caps and scarves into the air, shouting, "Hip hip hooray!"

Chapter XXX. Day One

Once George had disappeared Bobby sent people home. He and his mother went to Father Anselm's cottage to gather up his few things.

"I can't thank you enough, Father. As soon as I can I'll send some food to repay you for all the meals I ate."

"No need, Bobby," said Anselm. "It was a pleasure sharing my bread and pickles with you. That's how I knew you had actually changed."

Lady Nelda made a face. "The food at the castle isn't good, Bobby. I hope you like spinach."

Bobby gulped. He stuffed his spare socks and warm sweater into a bag and set out for home. The castle was in a sorry state. There were mossy stains running down beneath each window and weeds growing from the cracks between the stones. Lady Nelda took Bobby to the stable. Bobby's pony struggled to his feet to greet him. You could count its ribs.

"Cook and I have been pulling up tufts of dead grass from underneath the snow. That's all the horses have been getting." Bobby made a mental note to find some money.

They went through a side door into the kitchen. The Cook eyed Bobby nervously. "I've warmed up some dandelion greens, Madame. And because it's a special occasion, I baked a spinach pie." She smiled shyly. They sat down to lunch.

The Cook served the greens, then stepped back to await further instructions.

"Won't you sit down and eat?" Bobby asked the Cook. His mother gave him an angry look. The Cook herself looked shaken.

"Why no, sir. It's not my place." Lady Nelda smiled to hear the right answer.

"I don't see why. It's only dandelion greens," replied Bobby. "But do as you wish." He was hungry. He cleaned his plate. The Cook brought out a flat green spinach pie soaked in honey. Bobby and Lady Nelda pretended to like it. They thanked the Cook and urged her to take the leftovers to her children.

"Thanks, but I hate spinach pie," she said.

"Oh," they said, wishing the meal were over. When it was, Bobby gave the remains of the pie to his pony. Lady Nelda gave Bobby a lecture about servants.

"When you treat the cook as an equal you only embarrass her. She doesn't know how to use a fork. She doesn't know how to make polite conversation. She's much happier with her own kind. They talk about the weather, burp and pick their teeth with their knives."

Bobby knew that in some way his mother was right. But he had spinach stuck between his teeth, and wished he could pick them with his knife.

"Mum," he said, "do we have any money?"

"You'll have to ask Arno, dear – the Master of the Purse."

"Will he remember me?"

"He ought to. You once broke seven eggs on his head. Another time you bit his leg and it got infected."

"Oh," said Bobby and went off to look for him. He was glad to be back, though the castle looked emptier than he remembered. He found Arno in the castle office.

"Arno, I'm Bobby," he said in greeting. "Back in power."

"Oh, yes, your grace," said Arno, bowing. Arno's eyebrows were so pale they were almost invisible. They seemed to signal, "Not really," while the rest of his face said, "I'm afraid not."

Bobby asked for some money. "I'm sorry, your grace," said Arno. "The coffers are empty. It's all I can do to pay myself and the cook. I've had to sell some of the statues from the church."

Arno explained that the earldom got its money from the farmers. The farmers paid their taxes, called "rents," with bags of grain. Arno sold the grain to out-of-town dealers and used the money to pay the Earl's bills. To spite George, Alison had told Arno not to collect that year's taxes. Bobby couldn't ask the farmers for grain in planting season. They had only saved enough grain to use as seeds. All the rest had been ground into flour. There could be no rent collection till the fall harvest.

"Oh," said Bobby, thinking of the horses. "Don't we have any money saved up?"

Arno gave Bobby a look that meant, "Not really! I'm afraid not."

"So we can't hire anybody, or fix the castle?"

"Not until tax time, your grace."

"We've got to feed the horses. What else can we sell?"

"You could sell the horses. Then you wouldn't have to feed them."

Besides being mean, this idea was stupid. No one would want the horses in their present state. Bobby had an idea. "How about the old Earl's suit of armor?" It was rusting in a closet.

Arno's face said "Oh! I'm afraid not!" His mouth said, "Armor is made to measure. It wouldn't fit another man."

There was a long silence. Finally Arno spoke up. "Burgo, a merchant from Brown's Landing, wants to buy your forest. He would cut it down and cart the logs away. Alison wasn't interested."

"How much?" asked Bobby.

"He would pay by the wagonload of wood. Threepence per load, I believe."

"And how much money do we need to buy hay for the horses?"

"Let's see," said Arno, frowning. "At a penny a day . . . two months till they can graze outdoors . . . that's sixty pence . . . twenty loads of wood."

"Done!" said Bobby. "See that he cuts trees away from the road, out of sight."

"I'll do my best, milord," said Arno, although his face said something different.

Bobby heard the howl of a female voice. He followed the sound and found Alison in the kitchen.

"Hello, Alison," he said.

"I hate you!" she said. "You have no right to march in here and push everybody around!"

"All right," said Bobby. He wrapped a scarf around his neck, pulled on an extra jerkin, and left.

Alison followed him out the door. "Where are you going?"

"I don't know. Father Anselm's, I guess."

"Why did you come back?"

"I came back because it's home," said Bobby. "I've changed." He told her about Fahd, his travels, and the Great Deed. When Fahd was mentioned, a dreamy look came over Alison's face. She could hardly believe Bobby was Fahd's friend.

"Do you want your room back?" she asked with a pout.

"You can have it," said Bobby. "It's so wonderful having a bed, I'd sleep anywhere in the castle. By the way, George left for good. He has another wife in Shrewsbury. Father Anselm says your marriage wasn't legal. You're single again."

"Crikey!" said Alison. She became thoughtful. Then she hugged Bobby.

Chapter XXXI. A Better Bobby

Everyone went to bed in a hopeful mood. The next day Bobby went hunting. He shot arrows at two squirrels, a bunny and a blackbird. He missed them all, so he didn't have to fight with Alison about eating meat. He went to see Frog and traded some spinach for a turnip.

He broke it to Frog that the earldom had no money. Most of their plans would have to wait until tax time. He wouldn't be able to rehire the castle staff. He wouldn't be able to fix the roads, chase bandits or fight fires. He did, however, promise to be in the church every Thursday to hear complaints, judge disputes, and chat with people.

"I wonder," said Frog. "The old Earl used to schedule work days. Everybody had to go. One in winter, one in summer. The bailiff – Old Stout – would supervise. We hated it . . ." Frog stroked his chin. ". . . but we got a lot done. On the roads, especially. If everyone – or even just the ones who came out yesterday – put in a day of work, we could do a lot."

Bobby listened respectfully.

"I'll see what people think," said Frog.

Bobby smiled and shook Frog's hand. "Brilliant. *You* should be the earl."

Frog shook his head. "No thanks."

Bobby's reappearance in the village created a stir. The people who ran into him didn't know what to do. A man swept off his hat, a woman curtseyed, a boy bent one arm over his waist and bowed, a dog barked, an old woman retreated in embarrassment.

To each of them Bobby said, "Please, treat me just like any other neighbor. What's *your* name?" And he started getting to know people.

Lady Nelda thought Bobby should be more lordly. He disagreed. He felt the people liked and understood him. But his first public hearing in the church changed his mind. People whined, blustered, beat around the bush and even lied.

"High holiness! My Lord Bob! I am an honest tradesman, a dealer in pots and pans. I have done business up and down the High Road these past three years. I am known as a skillful hand and a straight shooter. But someone is trying to ruin me. A scheming, lying woman."

"And who would that be?"

"Her name is Everson, Sir, and a meaner, more conniving individual there never was . . . in England, on the moon or in hell." The man mewed like a cat in heat.

"Is she here?" asked Bobby. A sad woman with folded arms stood up. Bobby addressed her. "When this man is through you'll get a chance to speak." She nodded sadly. He signaled the man to continue.

"My Lord, this here Everson come to me in the weekly market to buy a stew pot. I show her a nice one. How much? Fourpence. She hands over the money. The one I show her is just a sample of my wares. I will deliver hers at the next market. She wants it now. She sets up a yowling and a chanting, a cursing and a dancing and calls me a cheat. Finally, though, she accepts my terms.

"Come next market, I am there with her stew pot. She picks it up, turns it over, taps it with a fingernail and screams, 'Thief! Arrest this man!' She claims the pot is thinner, smaller, and cruder than the one she saw the week before. She screams this to my fellow merchants and honored customers. Sir, I was deeply embarrassed.

"I offer to return her money. She wants the sample pot. My lord, how can I do business without samples? I tell her, 'I wants nothing but your satisfaction.' 'Marry me then,' she says. 'My child needs a daddy. On our wedding day I will accept this leaky piece of trash.'

"Now, I no longer had her fourpence. I had to buy more copper. 'All right,' I agree. 'I will marry you.'"

"'Good,' she says. 'And there's another thing. Climb Mount Baldy and whisper the magic spell that will improve the weather. Then fly up into the heavens, catch a Fluffy Bird and teach it to perform our wedding service in Latin.'"

"Do you see what is going on here, yer Eminence?" He tapped his forehead with a forefinger. "Nothing in there, Lord B!" Again he tapped his forehead.

Bobby was relieved that his first case was so easy. The tinker had tried to cheat the woman. He asked the woman for her side of the story. She spoke in an odd singsong.

"Cranbrook – this man here – asked me to wed. When's the wedding? He's trifling with me! He won't climb Baldy! Won't catch old Fluff! Springtime's overdue!" The woman started to flap her arms like a chicken.

Bobby interrupted her. "I order this man to give you his sample pot. Would that satisfy you, madam?"

The woman gave Bobby a hurt, confused look. The man shook his head, as if to say, "See?"

She started to yowl again. "Cranbrook! Fly to Everson. Fly, fly! Sing, O my beloved. Fold me in your arms! Then I will take your pot."

"Bring the sample pot here next week, Cranbrook," said Bobby. "Everson, come and get it then. That will be the end of this."

"Wait a minute there, Lord High Hill," said Cranbrook. "That's my sample. That's a beautiful piece of work. I won't let that go. That there was made by Pat of Pike. I could not replace that."

"Is that all I get, Lord High?" screeched Everson. "That won't warm my bed!"

Bobby threw up his hands. "I can't help. You'll have to work it out between yourselves. Next!"

The next case was a land dispute. Two farmers were claiming the same triangle of land with an oak tree on it. Each swore it had belonged to his father. Each seemed honest.

"Split the land between you," said Bobby wisely. "If you wish, I will come and draw the boundary."

"Arh, this won't do," said the first farmer, thrusting his chin in Bobby's face. "How much did he pay ye? Who put in the fix?"

The second farmer interrupted, "Aye, what kind of crooked deal is this? You're no angel, your Lordship! Yer a swine!"

The two farmers ran at each other and fought. When Bobby tried to separate them they both spat in his eye. He had to clear the room. He ended his first day as a judge with a bad success rate.

Chapter XXXII. Learning the Hard Way

Frog found that people were willing to work on the roads and ponds. Two days a year, as in the past. So Bobby and Frog walked the roads to see where repairs were needed. They chose a place with deep ruts and puddles. Bobby named a date for people to gather with shovels and rakes. Anyone who didn't come could do an extra day of work later in the year.

When the day came, Frog and Bobby were there early. Bobby brought drinking water and some spinach. Frog located gravel to fill potholes. He started leveling the ruts worn by wagon wheels. Bobby climbed a hill to look for his work crew.

Two hours later, nobody had come. Four hours later, Bobby and his helper ate some spinach and walked back to town. They stopped in a couple of farmhouses along the way to ask why no one came.

"I thought it was voluntary," said Diccon, a farmer they found repairing a length of rope. "Is there some punishment for not going?"

"Of course not!" said Frog. "It's not like the old days. You go because you want to."

"Oh, good," said Diccon.

They got the same answer from everyone they asked. "The old earl used to fine you if you didn't go. We like this new system better."

Frog was losing his temper. "What would it take to get you out to work?"

"The Earl would have to make us."

"But people want the roads fixed! They said they would come. Why didn't you?"

"I thought there would be plenty of people."

"Eesh!" said Frog. His face was red. His fists were clenched. He stormed away.

"I guess I'll have to force people," thought Bobby. That meant he would have to hire a sheriff. Arno would have to find some money.

In the meantime Burgo, the merchant from Brown's Landing, had started cutting trees. Wagonloads of logs, dragged by pairs of oxen, were creaking up the High Road. Bobby went to watch Burgo at work.

As he had asked, they left a wall of trees along the road. Farther back in the forest axe blows rang out, along with the crack of whips and shouts of "Timber!" There was a smell of freshly-cut wood. Bobby came upon a dozen woodsmen sharpening their axes, chopping trees, trimming off branches and guiding teams of horses.

One of the woodsmen trotted over to Bobby. "Get out of here. This is no place for a boy."

Bobby laughed. "I'm the earl. Burgo's paying me for this lumber. I came to see how it's going."

"Ah," said the man. "I'm Jack, Burgo's man. The trees are straight and tall, as we'd hoped. You'll do very well, Earl. Sixpence a load is good money."

"Sixpence a load?" thought Bobby with alarm. "Arno told me threepence. I'll look into this."

He went to the Office of the Purse. He found Arno building a model ship. "I've just been to the forest," Bobby announced. "The woodsmen are working hard. When will we get some money? The horses are hungry."

"I'll check with Burgo," said the Arno.

"Make sure he pays what he promised – threepence a load."

"I will!" said Arno. He smiled and returned to his model.

It looked as if the Master of the Purse meant to keep half the money for himself.

Bobby wished he didn't need a Master of the Purse. He could barely read and write, so he needed one. He invited Father Anselm to the castle to continue his reading lessons.

"C . . . a . . . t!" said Bobby, straining.

"Good!" said Father Anselm, pointing to another word.

"Heed!" said Bobby.

"Head," said Father Anselm.

"Oh," said Bobby.

Bobby could form crooked capital letters with his quill pen. He printed a sign for his bedroom door: "*Alisun kepe owt.*"

The reason for the sign was that Alison had a habit of complaining. She complained about her complexion. She complained that her breasts were too small and her legs were too fat. She complained that her hair was thin and straight. She complained that she didn't know any noble boys.

Bobby didn't blame her. She had had an unhappy childhood. Still, she was practically unbearable.

The old Bobby had tormented his mother. The new one was coming to appreciate her. It turned out her main interest was a card game called Old Maid. She couldn't do it alone, so she was always asking Bobby and Alison to play.

Bobby wished his mother could be more interesting – that she had traveled to London or even to France, that she knew the names of the birds, that she understood why apples floated and stones sank. Unfortunately, she didn't. All she knew about was fabrics.

Bobby found himself missing Fahd: their adventures, their little jokes, the feeling of satisfaction that the Great Deed had given him. Why can't an earl get that feeling?

Chapter XXXIII. The Fisherman Returns

About a month after Bobby's return an unfamiliar man walked up the castle drive. It was late March. Spring was in the air. The man was wearing a long gray robe and a felt hat with ear flaps. He whistled a cheerful tune. He had three fishing poles over his shoulder. He knocked on the front door. When no one answered he walked in.

"Hello!" he shouted. "Nelda? It's Arturo."

Bobby was in the Great Hall, working on his arithmetic. He rushed out. "Dad!"

"Bobby?" said his father cautiously.

"Welcome back," said Bobby. Arturo studied Bobby's face. He had heard that Bobby was different. But he didn't dare believe it.

"Thought I'd drop by," said Arturo. "See how you were all doing. Brought you some fish." He opened the wicker basket hanging from his belt and showed Bobby three silvery trout curled up on a bed of ferns.

"Hurray! Let's take them to Cook."

"Hurray?" thought Arturo. "That doesn't sound like Bobby."

In the kitchen they found Lady Nelda knitting some gloves, the Cook assembling a spinach pizza, and Alison gazing out the window.

"Arturo!" said Lady Nelda in surprise. "I thought you were a monk."

"I'm a friar," he answered. "But it's only for the fishing."

Alison stared out the window, ignoring them all.

"Look what he's brought us, Mum," said Bobby, opening his father's basket.

"Fish!" sang out Lady Nelda and the Cook. Now Alison started paying attention.

"Did you kill those?" she demanded.

"Yes," he answered.

"And how would you feel if a fish hooked you, dragged you into the water, smacked you dead and ate you?"

"I'd like to meet that fish," said Arturo.

"Ack!" said Alison. "We don't eat dead things! Do we, Mummy?"

Lady Nelda, who was smiling at the fish, didn't answer.

"Right, Bobby?"

Bobby was smiling too.

"Right, Cook?"

The Cook gazed at the trout and said, "They would taste mighty good fried in butter. Or poached in milk with dill and sorrel on top. Or baked with a mess of turnips. Or boned, cut into fingers, dipped in batter and deep-fried."

"You murderers!" cried Alison. Gathering up her skirts, she ran out the door into the forest. Those who were left behind scaled and cleaned the trout and grilled them in the fireplace.

"Place looks a bit rum," said Arturo as he picked the last fish bone out of his teeth.

"It is," said Lady Nelda. She told her husband the long story of Alison's marriage.

"Didn't like the fella," said Arturo. "Thought he was a bounder."

"He was!" said Bobby, and told about George's sour goodbye.

"So things are pretty much back the way they were?" inquired Arturo.

"Yes and no," answered Bobby. He told about his travels, his masquerade as the Royal Legate and his hopes of improving people's lives.

"By Jove!" was his father's reaction. "Working for the common good! Great!"

Bobby's heart was warming towards his father. He'd always taken him for a fool.

"And the Jester?"

"Went to London, so I've heard," said Lady Nelda

"The masters?"

"Gone, too, as part of Alison's budget cuts."

Arturo turned to Bobby. "Shall we start collecting taxes again at harvest time?"

Bobby's eyes lit up. "Just what I've been thinking!"

"Good," said his father. "And don't you think we can sort it out with Alison about the meat and fish?"

Bobby nodded vigorously.

"Good," said Arturo again. "If no one's been fishing around here there will be some beauties out there. I've got some useless old shirts and leggings in my closets. I'm sure there's a farmer who'll buy them. Shall we buy a goat?" And he went upstairs.

When Alison came back the family had a meeting. This had never happened during Bobby's earlier life. Alison was the only vote for vegetarianism. She gave in. The others could eat meat or fish as long as she didn't have to.

"Instead of looking like a beautiful garden," she sneered, "the dinner table will now be piled high with corpses. Hope you like that. Correction: hope you don't."

"Most people's tables look that way," said Bobby. "Including the best ones – the Count of Gambrell's for example." Bobby had a sudden inspiration. "Would you like to visit Gambrell?"

"Gambrell?" cried Alison in disbelief. "Home of the cutest boy in England? We could never visit Gambrell! They are far nobler than we are." Alison had heard about Tristan, the Count of Gambrell's eldest son, from a bishop who once stopped by for lunch. In her dreams, Tristan had blossomed into everything Bobby, George and her father were not: poetic, darkly handsome, quick to blush, eager to defend a girl's honor.

"The Count is sort of a friend," explained Bobby. "I think he'd be glad to see us. Not, however, if you criticize their diet."

Alison pouted. She couldn't be positive that the cutest boy in England was a vegetarian. "Oh, all right," she said. "But I'll need new clothes." She ran upstairs to go through her closets. She dreamed about Tristan. But she knew he wouldn't like her – a plain, poor, country girl. "Ack!" thought Alison.

Chapter XXXIV. Enter the Cutest Boy

First, Bobby had to notify the Count of Gambrell that he, Fahd's companion, was actually an earl. Then he had to get an invitation. He sent Father Anselm to make the arrangements.

Anselm came back a week later with an invitation to Gambrell for Easter. "The Count didn't understand what I was saying at first. He didn't have a clear picture of Bobby, or of having him thrashed. His Bailiff did, and feels very bad about it. His son, Lord Tristan, remembers Bobby perfectly. He took me aside and told me that Acton Waters is a swamp."

Bobby laughed. He had a feeling Tristan would be good for Alison. He wasn't sure why or how. When he relayed the Count's invitation to Lady Nelda and Alison, they went to work sewing new dresses and cloaks. They had little money, so they made new outfits out of old ones. They knew the Gambrell women would be wearing the latest London fashions.

An abbot passed through after visiting London. They peppered him with questions. Unfortunately, he only remembered what the priests and bishops had been wearing.

To bring out the purple notes in her hair, Alison soaked it in beet juice. It turned purple. So did her forehead and one of her ears. Luckily, the color faded before she left for Gambrell. Thanks to Burgo's lumber payments the family didn't have to walk. They had revived the horses. The lords of Brown's Landing and Beckham would be putting them up. Bobby sent word that he would like to visit the Vicar of Beckham, a man who had advised him to save his anger for wolves.

Spring was at its height when the family set out. Bobby's father led the way on his sleek brown stallion. He had two fishing rods slung from his saddle. Lady Nelda came next on her dappled gray. Then Alison in a complicated silk hat. She looked very nice, though she was already pink with embarrassment, imagining what Tristan would think of her. Bobby came along last on his prancing pony.

The farmers plowing their fields shouted cheerfully. "Bobby! You off somewhere?"

"To Gambrell," shouted Bobby. "So Lady Alison can meet the cutest boy in England!"

Alison turned red. She hissed at Bobby, "If you ever fall in love I'm going to make you so miserable!"

When they got to Brown's Landing, Bobby settled his family with Lord Brown and went straight to Pip and Prothero's house. They were delighted to see him in a fine suit of clothes and a feathered cap. He handed the boys a bundle. They tore it open.

"Toy soldiers!" said Pip.

"Little houses!" said Prothero. "Whose are they?"

"Yours," said Bobby. "I'm too big for them."

The boys hugged Bobby. Their parents hugged Bobby too. "You've had some luck, then, have you?" asked the father.

Bobby nodded and promised to visit again.

The next day wasn't quite as sunny. A passing rain left the family wet and shivering. They were happy to find a big fire blazing in the manor house at Beckham. Squire Brawley directed Bobby to the vicarage.

The door was answered by a tidy old lady. "Abel will be glad to see ye, I'm sure," she said, disappearing inside. The vicar wasn't sure who Bobby was until Bobby repeated the story of Red Bert.

"Ah yes," said the Vicar. "The angry boy. We ended as friends?"

Bobby laughed.

"You look happy. No wonder I didn't recognize you. Come in, come in," urged the Vicar. "We're just having some bread dipped in milk."

Bobby explained that he was needed elsewhere and handed the Vicar a package. The Vicar unwrapped it and took a deep breath.

"O my lands," he exclaimed. "A prayer book! Where did you get this, my lad?"

Bobby told a little bit of his story. He wanted the Vicar to know the book was really his to give, from his castle library. Tears appeared in the Vicar's eyes.

"I have only one book," he said. "A history of Mesopotamia. This makes me so happy."

"I'm glad you like it," said Bobby. "Thanks for being kind to me." He hugged the Vicar and went back to his family.

They were due at Gambrell the next day. Alison put on her finest dress, black velvet with a sprinkling of tiny pink bows. All day long she pinched her cheeks and chewed her lips to keep them red. Bobby wore his best outfit, too, so the Count and his family would know he was a nobleman.

It was late afternoon when Gambrell's church spire rose above the horizon. As they neared the town the road became more crowded. But the farmers and merchants gave them plenty of room. Alison in particular attracted attention. People praised her under their breaths. She noticed this, as she was meant to, and blushed.

At the edge of town they were met by the Sheriff, the man who had once invited Fahd and Bobby to sing at the castle. He was very polite, especially to Bobby. He took Arturo's horse by the bridle and led the family through town. The jostling crowds fell back, wondering who the Sheriff's guests might be.

The market square had been washed clean by spring rain. The Fortress of Gambrell had a comfortable look. There were flags waving from its towers. Bobby remembered Rembert and his men in this marketplace, waiting for midnight to storm the castle. Arturo wondered whether there were fish in the moat. Lady Nelda wished she had some money. Alison felt a mixture of excitement and fear.

Their horses thundered across the drawbridge. The big gates of the fortress swung open. Waiting inside was the Count and his family. Alison felt weak. She hardly dared to look. Lady Nelda instantly perceived that London fashions were not what she had guessed. She and Alison were in dark colors, without gloves. The Gambrell women wore light colors, puffed sleeves and gloves to the elbow.

The Count stepped forward. Bobby dismounted and embraced him. There was a pause while the Count revised his idea of Bobby. Now he recognized the insolent boy. But he reminded himself that Bobby was a minor nobleman who had helped save Medwick from Rembert.

Bobby turned to introduce his family. Alison was still trying to get off her horse. Her long skirt made this difficult. Finally one of the Count's men held up his arms and swung her to the ground. Her dress was rumpled, her hair was falling loose. Her face was scarlet and she was close to tears. In short, she looked like a 15-year-old girl. The Count was charmed and the Countess found her fresh and appealing. Lord Tristan shared a sneer with the girl standing next to him.

Now the Count introduced his family, which included children, sisters, brothers-in-law and cousins. When his eldest son, Tristan, was introduced, the boy did not step forward. He hung back with his head tipped to one side, appraising

Bobby and his family. Seeing this, Alison felt a sledge hammer to the heart. Tristan *was* darkly handsome, *was* beautifully dressed and groomed, and *did* look superior in every way. He also appeared to be on intimate terms with the girl on his right. She had silky blonde hair and a delicate profile. Her pale blue outfit complemented her blue eyes and rosy complexion. She was introduced as Lady Arabella of Nipkin, visiting from London. She looked about 16, straight and slender, a little taller than Tristan.

The Count led everyone inside. They went up to a sunny room furnished with Persian rugs and potted palms. They ate delicate snacks and made conversation. Alison had a hard time guessing which pastries contained meat and which did not. She had to spit out something she feared was chicken liver, trying to make it look as if she were wiping her mouth with her handkerchief.

An elderly gentleman whose name she did not catch tried to tell her London gossip. It seemed that the Countess of Nottingham was not speaking to the Marchioness of Bland because of something the Marchioness had said about the Countess's dog. Alison's eyes kept returning to Tristan, who was joking and flirting with Lady Arabella, poking her slender waist with his elbow and making her laugh. He was not conscious that Alison even existed.

XXXV. "Are you a vegetarian?"

At about six they retreated to their rooms. The castle had dozens of rooms. Every one had beautiful furniture, tapestries and rugs. Every one was lit with candles and warmed by a fire. Every one had a servant hovering near the door, waiting to be helpful. "A shave, milord? A nip of brandy? Shoeshine?" said Bobby's servant as Bobby approached his room.

"No, thanks," said Bobby. "I'm letting my beard grow."

Alison ran into her parents' room and sank to the floor. She wilted into a big circle formed by her black velvet skirt. "I'm not going to eat," she sobbed. "*She* is perfect. I am a mole rat."

"Aren't you hungry, Alison?" asked her father. "It's been hours since lunch. I'm starving." This unfeeling comment made Alison cry even harder. Nevertheless, when a servant marched through the hallways announcing dinner, Alison was so terrified of being left alone that she straggled along with the rest.

Bobby recognized the banquet room. He had been there before with Fahd. This time he was seated next to the Count. His father was on the other side. Lady Nelda and Alison sat on each side of the Countess, with Tristan next to Alison. Arabella was on Tristan's other side. When Tristan brushed Alison's elbow she almost fainted.

A dozen waiters ran in. First came the finger bowls. Alison thought it was soup, and was going to drink hers when she saw Tristan dabbling his fingers. The Countess asked Alison, "How was your trip?" Alison answered that they had stayed with the lords of Beckham and Brown's Landing and the weather had been good. The Countess smiled approvingly.

The Count asked Bobby about Fahd. Bobby told him about the happy marriage to Ennis. The Count smiled approvingly.

He had news of Rembert. "My cousin, the Duke of Northumberland, has reached Hungary on his way to the Holy Land. I just received a letter from him, written three months ago. Rembert and his men are damned resourceful. My brother has eaten venison and slept on a featherbed every night since he left England. If Rembert keeps this up, he may well be knighted."

Bobby raised his eyebrows. This was better news than he had dared to expect.

Lady Arabella leaned forward to stare at Alison's dress. "That's a lovely frock. Where did you get it?"

This was a moment Alison had dreaded. "My mother made it," she said into her lap.

"Oh, I was wondering," said Arabella. "I've never seen anything like it." She gave a little private glance at Tristan, who hunched his shoulders and snickered.

Now it was his turn. "Don't you love London?" he asked.

Alison was tempted to say yes, but didn't dare. "I've never been there," she said.

Tristan half-turned to Arabella and raised his eyebrows. She covered her mouth to suppress a giggle.

The waiters ran in with platters of squash, turnips, fried onions, grilled parsnips, haunches of venison, hams, a grilled lamb, quails, chickens, geese, ducks and animals Alison couldn't identify. There were bowls and pitchers of gravy, clarified butter, sour cream, chopped herbs, chives, dried apples and mushrooms. People tucked their handkerchiefs into their collars.

"This is by far the handsomest spread I have ever seen," said Arturo to the Count. "At our little place we count ourselves lucky to have two or three trout." The Count was not displeased to learn this.

Tristan mouthed the word "*stoo*-pid" to Arabella. She laughed out loud.

The servants bent over the diners. Alison knew she would look like a fool choosing nothing but vegetables. But what else could she do? She was sweating heavily. Soon there would be dark stains under each arm. The rosewater she had splashed herself with would never hide the smell. The trip to Gambrell was a complete disaster.

She stacked her plate with vegetables, hoping no one would notice the absence of meat. She sneaked a glance at Tristan's plate. It was almost empty. There was nothing but three lima beans, a dab of winter squash and a spoonful of sour cream. Could it be? Was it possible?

Almost in spite of herself, Alison spoke. "Are . . . are you a vegetarian?"

Tristan's face darkened. "How could that possibly concern *you*?"

"*I'm* a vegetarian," piped Alison, feeling utterly defenseless. Lady Arabella gave her a scowl of sheer hatred.

Tristan checked out her plate. His expression softened. "As it happens, I *am* a vegetarian. It's not because I disapprove of killing animals. I just don't happen to like the taste of meat."

"Oh," said Alison, dreading the next question.

"Why are *you* a vegetarian?" Tristan asked.

She lied. "It's just the taste I don't like, that's all." It occurred to her that Tristan might be lying too. She looked him straight in the eye. He met her gaze, then turned away in mild confusion. At that moment they became friends. Alison glanced over at Arabella's plate. Nothing but meat, a slice of each kind. Tristan noticed where Alison was looking. He gave her a conspiratorial look.

Alison relaxed. Two wet little half moons appeared on Arabella's pale blue bodice. Tristan began to show real curiosity about Alison and Acton Waters. Alison confessed that she had always hated Bobby.

"He does seem awfully satisfied with himself," said Tristan. The blood rushed to Alison's face. Tristan understood!

Arturo was having a lively discussion with the Count about fishing. His stay with the friars had made him a real expert. Bobby chatted with the Count's younger son, Tony, seated on his left. Tony had been thrilled by Rembert's raid. He wanted to hear about life in the robber camp. Lady Nelda found out from the Countess what they were actually wearing in London. The Countess confessed that she herself was far behind the times, and didn't care.

So the meal turned out to be quite a pleasure for everyone except Lady Arabella.

The next morning Tristan found Alison strolling in the courtyard. Although the day was cool, she was fanning herself.

"Have you seen Gambrell Town?" he asked.

"No," she answered simply. "This is my first visit."

He offered to show her around. "It's not much, but it has a certain rustic charm."

The two of them ventured out across the drawbridge. The square was empty except for a juggler, two beggars, and some women washing clothes at the public fountain.

Looking down from her high window, Lady Arabella saw them. She decided she had never liked Tristan and she hated the country. It smelled of manure, and no one knew French. She wept in sorrow and frustration. From another window

Bobby watched too, with amusement and surprise. It was not turning out as he had expected. But it was probably turning out better.

Alison went straight to the point. "I lied last night about why I don't eat meat. I . . . I don't believe in hurting any living thing – not even a fly." There was a long silence.

Finally Tristan spoke. "Well it sounds all wrong coming from the next Count of Gambrell, but I agree with you."

They walked along in step, not speaking, enjoying a moment of fellow feeling.

"This is a secret, you know," said Tristan finally. "I feel I can trust you." He looked her straight in the eye.

Their walk took them out of town, along narrow lanes lined by hedges, through blossoming orchards, around a beautiful pond whose calm surface reflected the sky. Tristan opened his heart to Alison. He always acted like a conceited snob because he felt it was expected of him, the next Count. Inside, he had serious doubts about many of the things his family took for granted. Slaughtering animals was only one example. He also had doubts about the Holy Trinity.

Alison recounted her own struggles. She reserved the story of George for their trip back to town. She could tell that Tristan saw her as an innocent girl. He thought nothing she had suffered could equal his own personal ordeal. And indeed, the story of her marriage cast her in a new light. She had endured trials far worse than any he could imagine. Though she was pretty and girlish, in some ways she was already a woman.

They kissed. Alison wept. Tristan promised to defend her forever, even if she forgot about him. They agreed that their friendship would be a secret. In public, they would pretend not to care about each other. Tristan promised to find a way to visit her in Acton Waters.

Almost everyone had a good time that weekend. Arturo gave the Count one of his best rods and took him fishing. The Count found fish where he had never even looked before, fish of a size and vigor beyond his wildest dreams. Lady Nelda taught the Countess to play Old Maid. Bobby went out hunting with Tony. Tony helped him with his archery, and on his last day Bobby wounded a duck.

It was Bobby's turn to invite the Gambrell family down to Acton Waters. But until he could raise some money, he didn't dare. Friendly though they were, they would probably get tired of spinach. He explained to the Count that things had gone downhill during his absence from home. He hoped within a year to have his earldom back in running order.

The Count wished him well and bade them all a warm good-bye. The Countess asked Lady Nelda to come back as soon as she could. Lady Arabella Nipkin wept bitter tears.

Chapter XXXVI. The High Road

Bobby's family headed south. But he rode north toward Creegan's Hollow, to visit Fahd and Ennis. He worried about his welcome from Ennis's mother. She thought their home was too shabby for an earl. When he got there he tethered his pony out of sight and changed into work clothes. Luckily, Rose of Sharon's warm feelings overpowered her shame.

"Bobby!" she cried at the sight of him, and folded him into her arms.

"You look fine," said Bobby. "Where are the others?"

"Ennis is out with the flock. William and Fahd rented some extra land this year. They're plowing. They'll all be home by dark."

Bobby strolled toward the high road, hoping to meet his friends. It felt good being a boy again. No one was waiting for him to decide anything. As the sky turned pink he heard a distant bell, a woman singing, and sheep. Within five minutes Ennis and her flock came into sight.

"Bobby!" She held his shoulders and gave him a sisterly look. Then she hugged him.

She penned the sheep. Then William and Fahd came striding along with shovels over their shoulders. They saw the pony first, and were mystified. Then Fahd caught sight of Bobby. He broke into a big smile.

"Ennis is having a baby!" he shouted. "If it's a girl, we're calling it Fara. That means 'happiness' in my language. If it's a boy we're calling it Bobby."

Bobby looked at his feet and swallowed hard. "Thanks, Fahd." They shook hands.

"Is that your pony, lad?" asked William. Bobby nodded. "It's a beautiful little thing. Let's get it unsaddled and into the shed."

That night, over a supper of leeks, spring greens and scrambled eggs, Bobby told what had happened in Acton Waters. They laughed at George and Alison's story. They thought Bobby's reforms might be taking things too far.

"Please teach this all to *our* squire," said William, laughing because he knew the squire would pay no attention. Fahd and Bobby sang their duet in Arabic. Fahd sang the Shepherdess Song he'd made up for Ennis. Then they all went to bed. The men had to get to the fields by dawn.

The next morning, after breakfast, Bobby stood up and gave a speech of thanks to Fahd. He apologized that he had brought them no money. He gave Fahd his pony.

"How will you get home?" laughed Fahd.

"The same way I did before," answered Bobby.

Fahd scratched his head. He looked at William, who seemed to be reading his mind. Finally he spoke. "It's very kind of you to give us your pony." All four members of the family nodded in agreement. "We wish we could use it, but it's too small to work on the farm, and we're too big to ride it. Take it home. When the baby gets big enough we'll come and visit you in the castle. We'll sleep on your feather beds, and eat roast beef, and feel pretty good about knowing an earl." Ennis put her hand on Bobby's head. Then she leaned down and kissed his hair.

Their faces were all aglow, except for Rose of Sharon, who swore she could never visit a castle. "I'm just a plain old shoe," she said. "I wouldn't know how to act."

Bobby told her that his castle was a drafty old barn, and the food was much better in Creegan's Hollow. She decided that she might go if William bought her a new shawl. Bobby kissed them, mounted his trusty pony and set off reluctantly toward home.

A fresh wind was blowing, ruffling the spring grass. Clouds veiled the pale blue sky. Partway to Gambrell Bobby found himself keeping pace with a woman on a high-stepping bay horse. Bobby was startled when a cultivated-sounding voice addressed him.

"What's a boy like you doing all alone?" The voice was low and melodious. She sounded young.

"I've been visiting friends," Bobby answered. "Now I'm going home."

"Home," said the woman with a sigh. "How do you like 'home'?"

Bobby sighed. "It's a fine place."

"I've had my fill of home," said the woman. "I'm going to London." Bobby looked up at her. She was beautiful. She was also a very good rider. He felt small and young.

She laughed. "Home is wonderful if you like smoky fireplaces and shepherd's pie. I like the city. It's dirty and busy and alive. Forgive me. My name is Angela – Dame Angela of Flitton."

"Bobby. Of Acton Waters."

"You look like a solid little person. Do you travel much?"

"Only to Medwick."

"Never to London, or Dublin, or France?" Bobby shook his head. "Yet you don't mind traveling by yourself?"

"No," said Bobby. "I've done a lot of walking, too."

"Well, what about London? Don't you feel a pull? Don't you want to see what boys do in the big city?"

Bobby confessed he was a little curious.

She pursed her lips. "Let me tell you about the City of London. King William built a fortress there called the Tower, because it's taller than you can imagine. It stands beside the River Thames, which is clogged with boats from all over the world. Walk along the river and you'll hear people speaking Ladino, Berber, Greek, Polish. The river is broad; London has the longest bridge in the world. Row up to the Strand, where lords and bishops live. Then comes the Abbey of Westminster, where kings are crowned. Next comes King Stephen's palace. In between, and all around, are warehouses, inns, offices, houses, workshops and markets.

"Anything and everything can be found in London. There's a Milk Street, a Bread Street, a Leathermarket Street, a Thread-needle Street. A flower market, a fish market, a bird market. Spices from Arabia, wine from Portugal, swords from Spain, monkeys from Africa, cheese from Flanders, dried fish from Norway. There are black men from Africa, Italians plucking mandolins, pale, solemn Danes. The streets are clogged with carts. Food, lumber and stone come in. And carts head out with barrels, boxes and bales of finished work. London builds ships, sings masses, trains horses, paints portraits, bakes cakes, sews shoes, brews beer, builds buildings. There are preachers, trumpeters, drovers, weavers, night soil men, sail makers, coopers and hatters. If London's too small for you, you can board a ship to Iceland, or Hamburg, or Gibraltar. What do you say, Bobby? Curious?"

"Ah," said Bobby, looking down the road ahead.

"I could use a boy like you. I'm tired of traveling alone. Let's go! Why not? My family has a grand house there."

Bobby couldn't tell whether she was serious. "I'll be happy to ride with you as far as Acton Waters, and lodge you for the night. My family will be delighted to meet you. For now at least, I'm needed in Acton Waters. I'm the earl. When I was away for a few months the place went to the dogs."

"How old are you?"

"Twelve."

"I like you better and better. Do you think you'll remember me? Will you at least come to visit? Flitton House, the Strand?"

Bobby looked up at her. "I hope so."

That night Bobby introduced Lady Angela to the Squire of Beckham. The next night they lodged with Lord Brown of Brown's Landing. Both were honored to have her as an overnight guest. Lord Brown pulled Bobby aside for a chat.

"Dame Angela of Flitton! How do you know her? She's famous! The Crown Prince himself is in love with her. But she'll have none of it. She rides by herself. They say she has a splendid castle up in Scotland!"

In Acton Waters, the sudden arrival of this exotic creature reduced Alison to tears. She was so beautiful, so self-assured, so refined! Within half an hour, however, they were friends. Lady Nelda was a little frightened of Angela. Arturo loved her. She had fished the Scottish burns, and invited him to visit!

When she left the next morning, Bobby went partway with her. They stopped at Frog's forge. A rhythmic clanging signaled he was in.

"Frog, this is Dame Angela. She's on her way to London. I've told her about the changes we're making. She wanted to meet you."

Frog scowled. "My hands are far too dirty to shake hands with you, or whatever I'm supposed to do." Angela laughed and curtseyed.

"You are the kind of man who makes our England England," she said, and kissed his leathery cheek.

Bobby escorted Angela to the edge of town. Before cantering off she flashed him a beautiful smile. "Don't forget! Flitton House!"

"I won't," he said.

On his way home Bobby stopped in at the forge. Frog looked up from his work, whistled and said, "That is the finest woman I ever hope to see."

Chapter XXXVII. Full Speed Ahead

Spring turned to summer. The harvest looked promising. It rained, but not too much. It was sunny, but never broiling. The crops shot up.

Bobby, his parents and Frog spent a couple of evenings figuring out how to collect taxes. They needed a sheriff. An outsider would be best, someone who wouldn't play favorites. Above all, he had to be honest. It was Arturo who thought of hiring a fisherman friar. The friars lived modestly, didn't marry and feared God.

Bobby, Frog and his father went to visit The Fighting Trout. They settled on a man named Finn who was tired of fishing. He was a big, hearty man who liked people. They hired him for two years. He promised to come to Acton Waters within a month.

Next Bobby dealt with Arno, the Master of the Purse. He found him in his office, gazing out the window.

Bobby came straight to the point. "Arno, I know you kept half of the money from Burgo's logging. Burgo's man says he paid sixpence a load, while you say threepence." This was a test he had devised for the Master of the Purse. If Arno confessed and handed over the money, Bobby would consider keeping him. At the very least, he would feel bad about firing him.

"Oh no, Earl," protested Arno. "I always said sixpence."

"I see," said Bobby. "You're fired. Before you leave, hand over the missing money. Otherwise I will spread the word up and down the land that you're a crook."

Arno put his head in his hands and wept. He went to his room and came back with a sack of gold. "This is all of it. You'll have to take my word for it. I know you can't count."

Bobby sat down and counted the money. Arno wept even harder when he saw this. His dream of starting his own restaurant was evaporating. The total was about right. Bobby told Arno to pack up and go.

Bobby called another meeting. Where should they look for a new Master of the Purse? Arturo suggested The Fighting Trout. Lady Nelda had a better idea.

"I'm good with numbers," she said, "and I've got plenty of time. I think I could handle the job. Could we keep Arno for another month, to show me the ropes?"

Everyone was delighted, including Arno. With harvest time just around the corner, Acton Waters was back in running order.

In the middle of July, when the first vegetables were ripe, Tristan of Gambrell and his brother Tony paid a surprise visit. They said they were just passing through, but they weren't in any hurry to leave. Tristan went on long rides with Alison, who told her family he was just a friend, nothing more. Tony learned the letters of the alphabet from Bobby. He taught Bobby how to hypnotize a chicken. When they finally rode away Alison cried. She claimed a gnat had flown into her eye.

Spring turned into a long, lazy summer. Bobby went fishing with his father, played Old Maid with his mother and listened to Alison complain about her complexion. Some afternoons he rode around the earldom visiting farmers and craftsmen. He watched them work and asked questions. "How do you keep the weeds down? Why do you dunk the red-hot horseshoe in water?" People always enjoyed explaining their work. He learned a lot. He continued his lessons with Father Anselm. He was starting to read and understand Latin, the language of the books in his library. He was getting big enough to graduate to a full-sized horse. His father taught him on a patient mare named Jenny.

But nothing exciting happened. Bobby spent a certain amount of time watching cows and goats. Farmers were now allowed to graze their animals on the castle grounds. Curious cowherds were always peeking in the windows.

Tax collection day came around on the first of October. Each farmer brought a measure of grain. Prosperous farmers brought two. Lady Nelda recorded the payments and Finn, the new sheriff, rode around making sure everyone paid up. By the end of the day several tons of wheat had been collected. Bobby turned the castle barn into a granary, an emergency supply in case of crop failure. His mother arranged to bag up and sell the rest.

The next day grain buyers came. Some bought a lot. Some bought a little. They loaded it in wagons and rumbled away on the High Road. Bobby ended up with a tidy sum of money, enough to rehire the orchestra, the juggler and the masters. But he didn't want a house full of entertainers. His family had new interests.

He hired a woman named Apple Annie to be market manager. She started collecting a penny's rent from sellers in the weekly market and used the money for upkeep. She made sure the merchants didn't cheat and were courteous to each other.

Once the harvest was in, Frog called a public meeting to discuss road repair. People agreed to work two days a year. The penalty for skipping was an extra pound of grain at tax time. On the first work day, a crew of almost a hundred men leveled a mile of High Road and trod gravel into it. Another crew cleared footpaths. Still another cleaned out the town well.

Slim the chimney sweep organized a volunteer fire company. Twenty people came to the first meeting. They asked

Bobby for money to buy leather buckets, shovels and a horse cart. Bobby was happy to comply.

It was time to work on Bobby's biggest project, the land exchange. To advise him, he called in ten of the best farmers. Finding a solution wasn't easy. Every plot was different – bigger or smaller, more or less fertile, closer to a stream or to a swamp, too shady or riddled with moles. Bobby's committee never figured out a workable plan. The land exchange was a good idea whose time was still to come. Bobby was disappointed by this failure. He had been counting on making things better and better. It turned out there was only so much he could do. By December his only active project was the Christmas Party. He wondered what was going on at Flitton House with Angela and the Crown Prince. "There *is* a way to find out," he said to himself. "Things have settled down here. Maybe it's time to go."

Chapter XXXVIII. Merry Christmas!

Alison was very active in the Christmas preparations. She was hoping Tristan would come. She made sure there would be good musicians, plenty of food, a flock of happy farmers and craftsmen, and not too much pear wine.

The previous Christmas had been bleak. This one would be the opposite. Arturo bagged a stag and some boars, which he left in the barn to freeze. He caught six salmon and had the cook smoke them. He bought two dozen chickens and three geese. The cook stocked up on mincemeat, apples, raisins, honey, cider, mead, and wine. She made plum puddings and set them in the larder to age. She ordered eggs for eggnog, butter for brandy butter and cream for trifle. She bought bacon, hams, sausages, cheeses, mushrooms, chestnuts, walnuts and filberts. There would be nut cakes for the vegetarians.

Bobby rode out with his father and felled three tall spruce trees. They set one up outside the castle door and two in the Great Hall. Alison decorated them with candles, strings of red berries and gilded pine cones. Bobby rode to Bradford Town to buy dolls and tops for the children.

Word went out that Christmas at the castle would be splendid. In the village and on the farms, people dug out their best clothes, mended the holes and roughened the shiny places with their fingernails. Children were taught manners. Father Anselm picked his twenty best singers to sing carols.

Bobby cut knotty pine torches in the woods. There were big torch holders in the Great Hall that hadn't been used since his grandfather's time. And he worked on a little speech he was planning to give.

Sure enough, Tristan and Tony appeared two days before Christmas. They were on their way somewhere else, but weren't needed for at least a week. The day before Christmas the band came to practice. Bead the Beadle had a little accordion. Arbuthnot, a farmer, blew a mournful krummhorn. Glider the coachman played the fiddle. Glider's wife, Annabeth, strummed chords on a battered lute. And Frog kept time with an iron triangle he had forged himself.

Christmas day dawned sunny and cold. A frozen crust on the snow threw back the glare of the sun. The first arrivals, a cluster of villagers, ventured up the drive in mid-afternoon. They were met at the door by Bobby himself and handed cups of hot mulled wine. They wandered through the castle, marveling at the tapestries and the tall windows, ending up in the Great Hall, where nuts and cheeses were already set out. Seeing them arrive, Father Anselm's chorus struck up the Cherry Tree Carol.

When darkness fell people were still arriving. The torches blazed up. The Hall was full. There were children playing tag, delighted by Bobby's little gifts. There were teenage girls leaning against each other and boys chuckling confidentially. There were farmers with broad red faces and thin, wor-ried-looking wives. Everybody had a plate, and every plate was full. Eyes were gleaming. Cheeks were shiny from the heat and excitement. The chatter was deafening.

After a while Bobby cleared out a space for dancing. The band struck up the Parson's Farewell. Couples formed and faced each other, Tristan and Alison among them. Tristan had eyes for no one but Alison. Alison knew where he was looking but kept her eyes lowered for fear she would break into a silly smile. They were light on their feet, afloat on a happy cloud.

People formed in rows for the Morris and Tom Tinker, and into circles for the Kettle Drum.

Arturo and Lady Nelda led the Mad Frolick, which speeded up until most of the dancers fell to the floor, laughing helplessly. Bobby chose that moment to step out and call for people's attention.

"It's wonderful having you all here."

Cries of "Hear, hear!" rose from the audience.

"I hope every Christmas will be like this from now on. I would like to thank all the people who are working for Acton Waters: Father Anselm, Finn, my family, the Land Exchange Committee, the volunteer firefighters, and most of all, Frog."

Frog tried to duck out of sight, but he couldn't miss the cheer that shook the hall.

Bobby continued, "I'm only a kid. I know how lucky I am to be at the center of all this. Everything's working out so well that I've run out of things to do. Traveling changed me for the better. Now I'd like to see London, and maybe cross the Channel too. I'd like to think you can't go on without me, but I know it isn't true. As long everyone here keeps working together, nothing will ever go wrong."

There was a hoot, and a growl, and they all found themselves cheering, because Bobby was right.

Lady Nelda dabbed at her eyes. "Bobby leaving, just when things were going so well?"

Arturo was thrilled, because Bobby's departure would give him a lot of responsibilities.

Alison didn't hear what Bobby said. In the crush of people she and Tristan were secretly holding hands.

Father Anselm was happy. He felt Bobby deserved some time off.

Frog was sorry to hear Bobby was leaving. But he wasn't surprised, because kids are always restless.

Everyone felt pretty good.

Bobby didn't leave until early spring. He traveled on foot. He couldn't afford to keep a horse in London. He couldn't afford to pay for food and lodging there, either. He took one gold coin, sewed into a glove, for emergencies.

He set out for London on a showery April day with a little pack on his back and a new set of clothes. He hugged everyone. Everyone cried. When he found himself alone on the high road, he broke into a grin and sang the Shepherdess's Song at the top of his lungs.